OCULAR PROOF

OCULAR PROOF

by
John Delacourt

Seraphim
EDITIONS

The publisher gratefully acknowledges the financial assistance of the Canada Council for the Arts and the Ontario Arts Council.

Library and Archives Canada Cataloguing in Publication

Delacourt, John, 1964-, author
    Ocular proof / by John Delacourt.

ISBN 978-1-927079-33-1 (pbk.)

    I. Title.

PS8607.E482546O29 2014   C813'.6   C2014-905514-5

Editor: Bernadette Rule
Author Photo: Andrea Stewart
Design and Typography: Rolf Busch

Published in 2014 by
Seraphim Editions
4456 Park Street
Niagara Falls, ON
L2P 2P6

Printed and bound in Canada

Quotations:

P. 4: "That pile of paper on his left was still alive ..."
       From Jean Cocteau, "La Leçon des cathédrales," in
       Poésie Critique, (Paris: Gallimard, 1959),
       vol. 1, pp. 131-132.

P. 14: "Under these circumstances the poems naturally
       formed no complete whole ..."
       From Jacob Burkhardt, "The Discovery of Man," in
       The Civilization of the Renaissance in Italy,
       (London: Penguin, 1990) p. 210.

P. 125: "I'll now proceed to argument and proof ..."
       From Lucretius (trans. Frank Copley), *On The Nature
       of Things*, Book iii, Lines 177-181 and 208-210, (New
       York: W.W. Norton and Co., 1977) p. 61.

In memoriam Michael J. McCarthy
(27 April, 1939 – 1 March, 2010)

And, as ever, for A.S. and my family.

Just a few weeks ago, I got a surprise in the mail: a postcard from a Canadian, of all things. Now you could say the fact I get any mail at all here at the cottage on this island is surprise enough. When the tourists are gone, it feels like there are just three goats and me this far out along the road, and they gave up on my company long ago. I never imagined I would live past eighty years of age, and I can count the people, still alive, that I write to on one hand. Well, one finger, really: my sister Olivia, still in London. But here it is, word from a Canadian apparently not even in Canada, judging by the card. It is from the National Gallery in Dublin; the image is a plate from Caravaggio's *The Taking of Christ*. It is postmarked from an address across the country rather than from Canada, and that is a little too near for a message like this from a stranger. The man's name on the card is Michael Tomassoni, and he is "looking into" – more like suspecting my involvement in – the disappearance of three works painted by his father Ranuccio Tomassoni. The paintings are mentioned in a catalogue from 1946 that his father still keeps with him among his few possessions.

So, how to reply. How do I begin to explain to this Michael Tomassoni all that went on during those years I knew his father and how much I regret what happened to that man? In these small, tightly packed block letters, the pen pressed down so forcefully on the postcard to form each word, there are a couple of sentences on the state of his father now. Ranuccio's memory is fading fast from Alzheimer's disease. He lives on the grounds of a monastery in Saskatchewan where he has worked as a kind of handyman and janitor for the last four years. It seems he had never settled for long in any place in his adopted country, never really found the kind of work or the kind of life that could replace what painting meant to him. He had taken up a brush once again several times over the years, only to abandon his paintings soon after. Michael Tomassoni has a very good idea of what lies at the heart of his father's tragedy of rootlessness and failure – the choice of postcard makes that very clear – but what does he expect from me? A confession? An acknowledgement of my share of responsibility for what happened to Ranuccio? An envelope with a cheque covering the amount these three paintings sold for in 1946? Maybe he just wants an invitation out to my home so we can talk about it all. He's traveled this far to Dublin, what's another drive across the country? I'm sorry, Michael Tomassoni. I can give you nothing but silence.

Well, until now, and now is twenty years after I have typed my last page here, put the work into this brown envelope and sent it off to my sister, with strict instructions to allow no one to break the seal before the date I have written under the title. Twenty years should ensure that no one mentioned, not even Olivia, will still be alive to read what is on these pages. She especially, the last surviving member of my family, should not have to answer any questions about this work and what I speak of here. There are still concerns of money and power involved in the story of Ranuccio Tomassoni's early painting career in Rome, his one gallery exhibition in Dublin and all that went on during those years. And we all know people can do terrible things when money and power are involved. So away this goes for a couple of decades, when I am sure my ashes will be long scattered deep below that ocean out there.

"That pile of paper on his left was still alive, like watches ticking on the wrists of dead soldiers." So said someone at Proust's funeral, speaking about that novel of his. Believe me, this is the only point of comparison I would ever make to Proust's work and the pages I now have ready for this envelope. Still, the truth is, for forty-six years I have waited for the ticking sound to stop, but it just seems louder than ever now.

And that is all very strange, given what is here. Most of these pages are taken up by a work in verse I completed in 1948 about the making of a counterfeit miracle during the Renaissance.

It would pass for what they call historical fiction, I suppose, the kind of novel that often gets written in the grey years when art, never mind politics, seems even more base and transactional than usual. I wrote this in Rome, Spoleto, Punta Massullo, and London, as one whole chapter of my life had concluded and another had yet to begin. Decades later, I can see it looks both backwards and forwards, from what I truly wanted to do with my life to what I became.

It looks backwards as I attempted to emulate Pushkin's *Eugene Onegin* with my own idiosyncratic version of that work's metre and verse structure. In my homage to one of my heroes I was testing what limited powers I had as a poet, to see if I could make of my writing more than a way to fill all those empty hours during the war. It is only now that I understand why I was so attracted to *Onegin*; so much of that work is about the tension between fiction and real life. And here I thought I was escaping myself each night as I plodded along writing verse after verse.

The work looks forward too, because the only work I did manage to publish in my lifetime was the book you may have looked up by now once you saw my name, *The Camera and the Photograph: Da Vinci's Shroud*. In this I proposed that Leonardo created the Shroud of Turin, "the first photograph," from his work with a camera obscura. Aside from library distribution, the publisher sold about one hundred and twenty copies, the majority of those at a "Believe It Or Not" convention in Phoenix, Arizona in 1975, where the book was displayed near a big seller called *Pyramid Power*. The secret of the pharaohs all too briefly worked a little of its magic for me too, I suppose.

As for this work, well, I know it is hard to read a long story in verse like this. If the artifice seems strange now, I can only imagine what it will be like twenty years from now. I am old enough to register the changes in the way people once talked, from the days of radio to the days of American movies to the days of American television everywhere. Yet the English language has never lost its strangeness for me anyway, despite my mother forcing me to speak

it from the age of four onwards, so there has never been a natural
register I felt comfortable with – whatever "natural" might mean.
No wonder it has been the language of my lies. Within its music the
simplest rhymes have always been irresistible. I knew, even when I
first wrote this work, the effect it would create for the reader would
be at best a smile of indulgence at a clever turn of phrase. If the
work was not going to "sound any depths of the soul," as my sister
Olivia not-quite-sarcastically phrased it, I would at least strive to
charm with the wit of a music hall comedian – a bit too broad, a bit
too fond of a trite simile or an easy phrase.

   And that's me through and through. Like a love of music hall
songs, such verse marked me as terminally second rate among the
more cunning and ambitious of my contemporaries at Cambridge.
They knew their Rimbaud and their Baudelaire. The more interesting and adventurous among them were deep into the work of such
strange new moderns of the time as Mandelstam and Mayakovsky.
The job was to come up with a harsher broken music of our very
own. They learned from acmeism and from Pound's imagism that
the work had to startle and compel a feeling that slipped through
the grate of polite impressions, no matter how resistant the reader
may be at first, and that a light, ironic tone was best kept for the
theatricals. Of course the inevitable result was that once I left Cambridge these same fellow classmen who had disparaged my work
and spoken of me as second rate found their métier and even their
fortunes peddling lighter entertainments and fiction, crafted as if
all of the technical innovation and the darker, dissonant chords in
composition were at best just an accent, like a sprinkle of sea salt
in candy.

   I was pegged as a callow aesthete. I knew my background
was only too questionable among the chosen ones. "That Kluge
fellow … hmmm … Russian, undoubtedly Jewish, though his
family would never admit it." At the root of it I was one of the
enemy, the philistines. I would never be anything else.

   Still I tried, upon graduation, to break into the writing racket.
I submitted my work to *The Criterion* and even received qualified

praise from Tom Eliot for a couple of poems. Yet nothing really ever came of it and I was barely scraping by, apprenticing on set design with the Old Vic Company. My father soon had enough of that and found a place for me in the London office of Vidler's as a porter in the artworks department.

Aestheticism became my last refuge. There is something very democratic about the whole culture of snobbery, of course. Anyone can attain it through received ideas. It takes no talent.

Though I always knew I would keep what you have here for the drawer, I had high hopes for my book on da Vinci. I thought it would dramatically alter the study of Renaissance painting and portraiture and our understanding of the artist. It would vault me into fame as an authentic art historian, one who no longer had to dirty his hands appraising work for Vidler's Auction House, where everyone knew I was only kept on because my father, Peter Kluge, had made Connie Vidler – or I suppose it is Sir Constant now – such a fortune with his antiquities acquisitions. I don't think I ever really got over the sneering indifference my book on da Vinci met with upon publication, the slow fade-out into obscurity it ensured for the essays I kept submitting to the *Journal for the Courtauld and Warburg Institutes* right up until Vidler's finally packed me off with a pension at seventy-five.

I have been on this island ever since. I received and entertained a few friends in the summer months over my first years here. And then less and less, as letters would come telling of who had passed away. I have traveled only for funerals over the last two years, it seems. I don't expect anyone to travel here for mine.

Here, in this package, is the last bit of business I must attend to before that day arrives. Once it is sealed and mailed off to London, at last the ticking of the watches will stop.

– Nicholas Kluge, Inis Mór, Ireland, 1994

Ocular Proof

"Be sure of it; give me the ocular proof." Othello 3.3.360

List of Characters

Niccolo Machiavelli	Amanuensis to Lorenzo de Medici
Franceschetto Cybo	Son of Pope Innocent VIII, husband of Maddalena de Medici
Bernardo di Niccolo Machiavelli	Father of Niccolo
Jacopo Corvo	
Pope Innocent VIII	
Cardinal Girolamo Basso della Rovere	
"Andalus"	Apprentice to Leonardo da Vinci
Lorenzo de Medici	
Leonardo da Vinci	
Maddalena de Medici	Daughter of Lorenzo, wife of Franceschetto
Jacopo Salviati	Citizen of Florence
Pico della Mirandola	Academician, member of Lorenzo's court
Ludovico Sforza	Duke of Milan, Leonardo's patron
The Actor	
Gethsemane	Alchemist and "witch"
Fabrizio	Trader in relics, objects from the Holy Land

Ocular Proof takes place over the course of the summer of 1491 in Milan.

A note about this list of characters:

The one major difference between this novel in verse and my published work The Camera and the Photograph: Da Vinci's Shroud *was my interest in Niccolo Machiavelli. I have gone through my old notes and found a letter to my sister Olivia, my first reader, where I said I had been reading a lot of him, specifically his plays, and I believed the war put a lot of his work in a new light for me. What I should have written was that I realized the war had made a Machiavellian out of me. I identified with the version of him in those pages: a marginal character, impressionable, an errand boy learning to be a fixer.*

Yet there are other characters that, over time, have revealed themselves to be shaped by those that made up my life in Rome during those days. I see a lot of the art dealer and gallery owner Harry Maes in how I wrote Leonardo and Lorenzo, a lot of my friend Antony Farrell, archivist at the Vatican Library, in Lorenzo's view of how art could be "useful." What I imagined of my sister Olivia's horrible marriage to the Irish playwright Martin O'Reilly has made its way into the characters of Maddalena and Franceschetto Cybo. Innocent's cynicism and corruption was influenced, in equal measure, from my dealings with Connie Vidler and what I knew of the inner circle of Pope Pius XII. And there are others who will no doubt come to mind as I read this one last time.

For Michael Tomassoni, there is a fair amount of his father in this Andalus character. Andalus never existed but he should have, much in the way Ranuccio Tomassoni should never have been completely forgotten or erased from this particular history, as a few peripheral characters in my life assured me he was.

So many omissions from the official history. Wisdom might mean nothing more than knowing what they are, and that there is nothing one can do about them. Save write something like this, for better or worse.

1
Introduction

A dedication to Niccolo and a brief description of his lost work.

He wrote of fathers later on
From all the extant works we have
Uncovered, though so much is gone,
So much he deemed unfit to save,
His gift he'd later dub a curse;
The more the muse required, the worse
The wounds of circumstance would bleed
Upon the page, the words he'd read
Which first he wrote to trap the light
Of truth's chiaroscuro shades
Revealed in those with fortunes made
In state affairs, where wit trumps might
And virtue falls to baser drives.
He truly understood their lives.

*When my father Pyotr Kluger (the name is from Galicia originally)
finally decided it might be wise to leave St. Petersburg in 1917, I was old
enough to sense that all the trunks weren't being packed for the harsh sun
I remembered of Odessa. This would be different. On a summer night
out on the terrace of the old family home I watched my mother Sofia sew
earrings and two necklaces into the hem of her overcoat – a memory that*

now I still cannot quite believe, but yes, people did such things. Memories like these serve to me remind me that, my God, I'm old.

My father had spent the first thirty years of his life in St. Petersburg moving up through the ranks of the Czar's military academy, eventually becoming a colonel in the Corps of Engineers. He fenced well, he rode well, while all the time cultivating the persona of some young bohemian drawn to painting and music and theatre because of his weakness for all the bad influences that corrupted the best officers. Even though he couldn't advance any further, he simply would not believe Nicholas and his inner circle would hold him back because he was Jewish. Such was his loyalty that when Nicholas abdicated, my father figured his time was up as well.

He took the family to London and he became Peter Kluge. He dropped the 'r' from our name because he presumed it sounded too Jewish and Kluge would simply read as German. He told anyone who asked that he wanted Olivia and me to be raised in the land of Shakespeare, not in the lands of Goethe or Voltaire (though the fact that Uncle Theodore had seen his jewelry shop in London flourish for over thirty years, ensuring we would settle in reasonably well, was closer to the truth). My father imagined that, for the last half of his life, he would gradually work his way up the rungs of London society to become the kind of Russian Jew the working class would despise.

That was quite an aspiration for the time, plausible as long as one doesn't have to worry about employment or dealing with the realities of always being seen as an upstart and outsider. I have become reconciled with my father's struggle for respect as a lackey for Connie – or I suppose I should get used to saying "Sir Constant" – Vidler and the auction house's various interests abroad. I realize now he was actually quite fortunate that Vidler had seen something in him and kept him working long after he had proven his limited usefulness – just as I was kept on well past my better days.

And this was more a threat than cause
To celebrate, when one is bound
To serve, in spirit of the laws,
Yet at the pleasure of those found
To live above such harsh dictates.
They soon enough found cause to hate
The beauty of the telling phrase
The way that character betrays
All veiled designs and subtle tricks
Within the plays he wrote to please.
Where laughter is but brief release,
The thorns of faith retain their pricks.
His vision proved subversive, stark,
A wisp of flame to pierce the dark.

And so, just like an architect
Who'd rather sketch the perfect line
That arcs and will not intersect
To serve conventional design,
He penned a treatise which he called
"On Revenge," but then, unsold,
Unread, he kept it to himself,
As hidden as ill-gotten wealth.
In it he writes of fathers who
Enlist their sons as soldiers for
The cause of settling a score,
Injustices they'd felt accrue
And shouldered stoically for years.
The ledger is the boy's to clear.

And yet, what makes a son be deemed
As good or bad is less about
How virtue served the world or seemed
To banish any cause to doubt
The motives of a paragon.
The cruel truth was that anyone

Could have their goodness come to naught
And, with a clarity of thought
That purges all his skeptic's pride
(the work is spiked with irony)
The author seems to smile when he
Declares that there's a slight divide
Between the towering heights of fame
And fortune's barren plains of shame.

Yes, shame is really what this work,
For all its artfulness, concerns,
The way the prince within the clerk
Must not reveal the way it burns
Yet try to let it stoke the fire
Which fuels the heart that never tires
Instead of blackening the soul
And hardening him within a role
Of introspective, humourless
Aggrievement with the fortunate
Who seem so poised, legitimate
In their much coveted success,
For if our lives confound each plot
We shape, revenge is best unthought.

It's difficult to read it now
And not detect within the prose
His ancient influences, how
The aphorisms sound so close
To Seneca's – that gimlet-eyed
Asperity that will not side
With unexamined sentiment,
Trusts what is done, not simply meant.
With acts heroic or debased
Are pentimenti that suggest
The self's a kind of palimpsest
Defined as much by what's erased

As what is proudly on display –
We never know what we portray.

This truth, so stark upon the page
Is really better understood
Within his writing for the stage.
Creating characters, he could
Effectively depict that strange
And subtle alchemy of change
That works upon each living soul,
The turns in plot that take their toll,
Reducing all the elegant
Designs of self-belief to just
An edifice that turns to dust
And rendering irrelevant
The rage against that tragic weight
Of time's imprint, the force of fate.

As a young man working for Vidler's in Rome, I, out of necessity, had set myself the task of analyzing the pigments of paintings assigned to the fifteenth and sixteenth centuries. It was then I met Antony Farrell, who was working in the Vatican library as an archivist (why I never seemed to question our chance meeting speaks of my naivete, the perpetual state of innocence I kept myself in). Antony encouraged me to look into the study of alchemy, because so much of the creation of pigments came from these hermetic texts. I realize this is now a firmly established basis for research but at the time such an approach was at best unorthodox; the damning adjective my father put down in a letter to me, from Istanbul, where he was then based, was "adventurous."

Yet I wagered that Connie Vidler would be open to my arcane ideas. High stakes indeed, putting both my own career and probably my father's on the line for the task at hand (determining what was real and what was fake in a whole estate's worth of artwork in Naples – one of my first big jobs), yet there was something in the fakery of alchemy, in its melodramatic occultism, that appealed to Connie Vidler. He came, over the years, to feel that I had saved his name and business at a crucial time after the war and that this bold approach spoke well of my instincts.

Ocular is steeped in all of those esoteric alchemical references, I know. I was such an earnest student, and I felt I had to prove I understood its first principles. My ideal reader at the time was probably Antony Farrell. He has been practically the only reader, aside from my sister, until now.

2

The Frieze

PART I

An introduction to Franceschetto Cybo, son of
Pope Innocent VIII and husband of Maddalena de Medici, with some
words on his importance to both families.

I told myself what I wanted to achieve by introducing these characters in
the opening four chapters was the creation of a kind of frieze, inspired by
a quotation from Burkhardt, from his Civilization of the Renaissance
in Italy, *on poetic development from the canzoni form.*

"Under these circumstances the poems naturally formed no complete whole, and might just as well be half or twice as long as they now are. Their composition is not that of a great historical picture, but rather that of a frieze, or of some rich festoon entwined among groups of picturesque figures. And precisely as in the figures or tendrils of a frieze we do not look for minuteness of execution in the individual forms, or for distant perspectives and different planes, so we must expect little of the kind from these poems."

Well, what follows are 'picturesque figures,' anyway.

When Franceschetto Cybo reached
The age when he could start to plan
His life, he timidly beseeched
His father for a man-to-man
Discussion of the terms of their

Relationship and finally aired
What since he was a child he'd feared:
He'd be disowned, no father's tears.
For, born an unacknowledged child
Of one who chose as Pope the name
Of Innocent, who made his fame
Before his office for his wild,
Debauched embodiment of all
Declaimed as cause for Rome to fall ...

Just made it more integral for
His claim to credibility
To place a wall without a door
Between the way he used to be
And what, in finest robes of white
He claimed, both wooden and contrite,
To have become upon the throne.
So bastard sons were on their own.
And yet this father realized
That Franceschetto's talents were
Beyond the gifts he could confer.
In ways the Pope was well advised
To keep within his arsenal
A force unschooled and prodigal.

For Innocent became the Pope
As victor in the war between
Two rival factions. Now his hope
Was that he'd quell the Florentine
Cabal of one Della Rovere
Who had, since thwarted, put on airs
Of one usurped by votes that cost,
In coins of gold, a fortune lost
For Innocent, and now, exiled
As Cardinal in Florence, seemed
Content to wait, and slowly schemed

Against a Vatican defiled,
Impoverished and torn apart,
With nothing sacred but its art.

With such a threat, the choice was now
For Innocent to hold his throne.
He had to realize just how
He'd face his options on his own:
To fill the coffers that were bare
Or meet his fate in grave despair,
One sure to face a brutal end,
No allies left who could defend
Him, given that his power relied
Upon his gift for alchemy,
Transmuting every enemy
Into a wealthy man, on side
For the designs of his empire –
A war was all it would require.

In my notes from this time: "I want to evoke the sudden development of dramaturgy and perspective that occurs during this period. I'll create a marked transition where static perspectives become dynamic as they become embedded in a narrative, and the frieze comes to life." I was already writing commentary for posterity, it seems, preening for an invisible audience.

The first figure here is Franceschetto Cybo, the illegitimate son of Pope Innocent VIII. So much of what occurs in Ocular *centers around the decisions and direction of Lorenzo de Medici, by all accounts the model for Machiavelli's Prince. Yet in my theme and plotting I wanted to present in Cybo's character a strong counterweight, a kind of photonegative of how power and authority was exercised. I wanted Cybo's story to be the corrective to all the kitsch about Lorenzo heralding a golden age. Cybo was just as much a creation of these times.*

As his kind was all too common in mine. When I hear the old snobs still working at Vidler's complain about the vulgarians they must deal with – inevitably with some racist remark about the Saudi, the Indian, the Chinese in London shopping in Knightsbridge and looking for the gaudiest trinkets and the loudest, logo-emblazoned clothing that can declare their new wealth to the world – the underlying argument about this "primitive" sort of client (as Connie Vidler's daughter called them – oh Lucy, you never really knew your father) is that they typify the steady decline in culture and values here in Europe. Apparently it really all began with Maggie Thatcher.

I don't even bother to argue with them anymore, tell them about the Barone Lanza di Strabias and the Marquesa Contis of King Umberto's court during Mussolini's years in power, the dark comedy of their embrace of the modern in all its sleek, chrome-plated emptiness. There were too many models for Cybo's thuggishness among the trumped-up minor aristocrats racing their motorcycles out on the dirt tracks by the factories, with their amphetamine addictions, their love of American prize fighting and "negro" dancing. Cybo the prodigal was my contemporary.

For every campaign waged in lands
Unknown to most brings great success.
The poorest soldier understands
The more he plunders there, the less
His glory fades on his return.
Nobility was his to earn
And riches from each dark crusade
Would etch the map in routes of trade
Through cities of the Caliphate
Where so much of the ancient world
Was just a tapestry unfurled
To please a prince and educate
The brotherhood in pagan thought
Concealed in texts covertly taught.

Such plans required complicity
With houses that had much to gain
From conquest and duplicity

For private wealth and power attained
Where Innocent had cause to hope
Medici would support a Pope.
Lorenzo had in his designs
A wish to join two family lines
By offering his daughter to
This bastard Franceschetto's arms,
With a belief a woman's charms
Could mend a broken soul anew.
It was a pact that needed just
The Church's blessing and its trust.

Yet any expedition planned
And sanctioned by the Holy See
Was simpler when the foreign land
Assured an easy victory.
That quickly changed when forces of
The Ottomans attacked above
The latitudes within the realm
Of Rome and seemed to overwhelm
Otranto's battlements without
Enormous losses to their fleet.
Within just days came a complete
Surrender of this old redoubt.
The wise in Rome knew such a threat
Might force a war all would regret.

A culture of defence prevailed
Where those who harboured grand designs
For empire's increase simply failed
To move those on the battle lines.
But once Otranto was reclaimed
The pagan roots of faith were blamed
For weakening the church's hold
Upon the flock. The clerics told
Of parables of Babylon

Rewritten like a book of hours
From ancient sources, occult powers
To paint a godless pantheon
Within the mind of every man –
Rome had to show it took a stand.

And still the curia would sell
Indulgences to those who had
Grave fears that they were bound for hell.
Expensive guilt sufficed to pad
The figure of the Church's wealth,
Accounts infused with spiritual health
Replenished by a Papal nod
And one lump sum to square with God.
The litany of compromise,
The principles debased, told in
Confessionals, to air each sin
Concealed in sharply fashioned lies,
Worn for the world like widow's weeds
To mourn the soul's claim to its deeds

Would prove a most effective means
For Innocent to proudly claim
His talents shone behind the scenes
To batten throne and shun the fame
Of those before him who would play
The humble saint, who turned away
From worldly gain to dedicate
His life to those less fortunate.
Best leave the theatre to those
Who felt the need to sway the crowd.
All he required was an avowed
Defender of his realm. He chose
Franceschetto to secure
Alliances new arms ensured.

All these years later, I read "Best leave the theatre to those / Who felt the need to sway the crowd" *as a dig at my sister Olivia, who had just had her first successes with the RSC as Katherine in* Henry V. *I was jealous, catty, resentful of the freedom she was allowed because our mother and father just presumed she would be on stage for a few years before she married well. Had I known what the pursuit of her career would cost her over the years or what an act of theatre my more conventional line of work would become, perhaps I would have chosen different lines here.*

He gave his boy the power to build
A force that could police the states,
A threadbare rationale distilled
From this corrupt pontificate's
Belief that if an enemy
Could be declared, its infamy
Lay in its power to be concealed
Within the feminine, revealed
By practices occult, profane,
A lustful nature, welcoming
The way the fallen angel's wing
Would cloak at night the mortal stain
From base desires that lay within
Each woman's love of carnal sin.

The worst of these had secret ways
To purge the living consequence
Of appetites the heart betrays
Where virtue offers no defence.
The power they had could undermine
The church's claim to grand design
By exercising such control
Of transmutations of the soul
Made real, just like the sacrament,
Through alchemy and arcane rite,

Strange liturgies they would recite,
Enrapt in dark experiment,
Such women were identified
As heresy personified.

So suddenly this reprobate
Who, since he was a bastard child
Had found no cause to demonstrate
He would in time outgrow his wild,
Impetuous impulses to
Map vice's darkened avenues,
Or cultivate himself beyond
The few pursuits that he was fond
Of – gambling, brawling, drinking, and
His masquerading as a prince,
Had gained the power to convince
The sycophants of Rome who'd stand
To win the most from his dark deeds.
Each empire sanctions what it needs.

If he could manage to portray
In married life the figure of
A man once lost who found his way
Again through his belief in love,
As credible as nuptials were
Within this world, who would deter
The daughter of Lorenzo – this
Sweet Maddalena's wedded bliss,
If bliss itself could be defined
As mutual relief from fear?
Each family's power was but a mere
Bright flash before a slow decline
From great prestige and influence
To jaded nights of decadence.

So much of this plot comes down to Antony Farrell – whom I have really not thought about for a decade or more. Antony, the ex-priest who came out of All Souls and just magically found himself with champions and supporters within the Curia who had secured his position.

We met through Harry, who had known Antony for some time. Harry was like the art world's courtier for those mandarins who professed their love of art in Mussolini's government, so it was inevitable that Farrell would find a way to charm himself into his circle, without anyone ever figuring out how he got there in the first place. Antony had a fine and supple mind and an innate understanding of power and politics. He had that dancer's physique and the soft, chestnut coloured hair with the Clark Gable forelock that would have made him almost dashing and elegant if he hadn't been so slyly self-effacing. Yet there was something else too, something half-starved in him. His eyes lit up at life then flickered out quickly, as if he could not regenerate the battery power in his soul.

I was stand-offish with him at first when we met at a private dinner of Harry's in Milan, just before one of his vernissages. Farrell was so brilliant, Harry said. He knew so much about Old Masters. Well, if he was so brilliant and charming, I had thought, surely he'll come to me and show an interest in what I do. And he never did. Yet the sly grins we shared at the dinner table and the roll of the eyes at what some old pedant would say were enough for me to believe Antony was at least an ally.

It was the work that really brought us together. There were moments throughout the two or three years we were engaged with "the Othello project" for MI6 that we could both share our doubts, our incredulousness at some of the demands we were working under.

In time Farrell trusted me enough to tell me how the Othello project came into being. There were two Irishmen among the Curial staff at the Vatican, working under the Cardinal Secretary of State: Dermot Quigley and Bernard Delegarde. I had only met them briefly in the winter of '41 and I'm sure that was how they preferred it, given their plans. Antony said he owed Delegarde everything for how he found him the archivist's position at the Vatican. "Barney," who looked like the spawn of an Irish priest and a bulldog, had been there for Antony from the moment he left the priesthood. I considered it best not to ask why. Delegarde and Quigley – who was always badly shaven, his olive skin nicked from his cheeks to his neck – were a kind of Rosenkrantz and Guildenstern in the end, sent out on a fool's errand from those higher up within the Curia, whom they would never speak about. They needed a "boy on the ground" to liaise with MI6 and the painters involved, and to ensure there was at no time a risk about the absolute secrecy of the project. That secrecy was less about the risks involved in the public finding out than the Vatican itself. Barney knew that only a fallen priest like Antony could take on that role because, at the root of it, the Othello Project was a plan to undermine Pius and risk not only his position but his life, to save the greatest paintings in the Vatican's possession.

Pius, for all his celebrated skills as a diplomat was, as Antony described him, "a problem." Quigley and Delegarde could barely speak of him without muttering profanities. The Curia had watched Pius entertain Hitler's errand boys, allowing Goebbels a private audience and a tour of the Vatican's portrait collection, and they knew the Pope was less of a diplomat than a useful idiot who was naïve about how far the Nazis would go in their demands for complicity. Those who took care of the artwork had no illusions about Goebbels's interest in the paintings. Hitler's "Heritage Department" had plans for amassing the greatest collection of artworks possible for relocation to Germania, and the Vatican would certainly not be spared. Whether Pius was oblivious or at heart complicit did not matter in the end; something had to be done.

I always figured it was Harry who made Quigley and Delegarde aware of me and the services I might offer. Yet years later, over a drink in London, Antony told me that MI6 actually reached out to Connie Vidler first and he was the one who pulled me in, knew who to bribe so I could get the right visa to stay in Rome. Sir Constant clearly intuited something about the Kluge ambition, how both my father and I had a talent for shape-shifting.

And so it came to be then, from
Such little expectation that
This Franceschetto would become
A man of substance. So much sat
Upon his shoulders now to bear
Than simply fathering an heir
That would enfold the Holy See
Within the principality
The House of Medici could claim.
However, he (dimly) seemed aware
This cabal of della Rovere
Had interests also in this game,
Would plot his possible demise
With regular reports from spies.

No one among the court of Rome
Would he entrust with what was shared
Within the walls of any home.
Built from these fragile bonds, he aired
The thoughts and fears that haunted him
As soon as sunlit rooms would dim
Among his troupe of sycophants
And parasites that knew the dance
Of servitude within the tune
Whose cadence was camaraderie
Despite the chords of misery
That underscored his picayune
Accounts of minor battles won
(In this he was his father's son).

He truly was a man made for
His times, despite what some would say
That to be schooled in love, not war
And to be cultured in the way
That one could quote the ancients, trill
The sweetest melodies, yet fill

An adversary's heart with fear
The instant when it became clear
One's name and honour were at stake
Was to be favoured in an age
When in the square, or on the stage
Each man seemed almost free to make
If not a prince, a courtier of
Himself – when fortunate in love.

Yet love had never been a part
Of any schooling he had done.
Whatever stirred within his heart,
Just like his claim to be the son
Of Innocent had been denied
Legitimacy, so he tried
To cultivate a common touch
Allowing him to show not much
Of interest in a life beyond
What gratified the basest drives.
Within this underworld he thrived,
Found meaning in fraternal bonds
Among the battle-hardened men
Whom, Roman born, Rome would defend.

By the time I had begun Ocular Proof *I was really looking back into my own years in a kind of underworld. The moment of my initiation was when I met Harry Maes, an art dealer who became famous for the network of art forgers he kept commissioned during the war for work he sold to the Nazis.*

This all eventually caught up with him and he was tried, imprisoned, and executed in Berlin for acts of treason against the Reich. This was a charge he also could have faced in Britain, given what he divulged of the plot Antony Farrell and I became involved in. Yet if Harry was guilty of anything, it was his deep understanding that every belief or ideology or faith had become, like the artwork he peddled, simply transactional in value. In another time, Harry would have been an artist himself, but he had put his shape-shifting skills to use as a kind of nihilistic experiment to see how far he could go. These conceptual artists now that claim Duchamp as one of their forefathers, they should really look to men like Harry. He could have done as much or more to change the game of the art world, had he lived.

There was some question as to whether Harry Maes was his real name at all. I had heard he'd taken the name Harry from Harry Kessler, the art collector and part-time diplomat for Germany who became the "Red Count." Maes was one of Kessler's boys, they said, and Kessler always considered it his mission to give these brief flings of his some culture. Maes was, as they say, an apt pupil.

He spent the years after the Great War in Antwerp, then in Amsterdam, an actor and director and then an impresario who mixed among a few interesting painters and composers and con men. All of them made it through the Second World War and wandered from city to city, staying off the street by doing whatever hackwork they could carry off. I remember turning on the television late at night in a hotel in Zurich, this must have been '74 or '75, and there on the screen, in some horrible American movie, was one of them that Harry had introduced to me at an exhibition, with a speaking part as a Nazi. Harry would have survived the war as well, I'm sure, had he not been the one among his group who proved useful to the powerful.

By 1935, Studio Maes in Milan had exhibited some of the most successful of the painters and sculptors Il Duce's regime considered fit for purchase. You would be wrong to imagine this was all forgettable work. There was a Morandi, a Carra, a di Chirico show. Even Tamara de Lempicka sold well, with Harry as her dutiful and faithful champion.

Yet Harry was not one to trust his run of luck in Italy. One of his better customers had told him about a certain circle of collectors and self-styled connoisseurs in Germany, newly moneyed and eager to outdo each other, who were looking for work of the great Dutch and German masters of the Northern Renaissance. The Fuhrer himself, he was told, no matter how philistine his tastes were about contemporary work, had an eye for Rembrandts and Vermeers, and if one was ambitious and

*well connected, it was a very wise move indeed to be considered a man
of taste in the failed painter's eyes. Harry's bold, brilliant idea was to
establish a secret network of painters from all over the continent that
could supply these new "connoisseurs" with a flawless collection of fakes
on demand.*

*In 1942, when I first met him in the St. Regis Hotel in Rome, he
had just begun to deal with these wealthy Germans who wanted "real
art, not the degenerate shit you get in Berlin." I immediately liked the
look of him with his auburn hair pomaded just like Fred Astaire's, his
tailored dinner jacket, the rose in his lapel. He knew I was in the market
for a certain client and rhymed off what was on offer. He could get me
a Vermeer from an old Dutch friend of his working out of Rocquebrun,
a Hals from this fat old Marxist who had relocated to Hamburg. Even
a Raphael, lost for generations, could be "rediscovered," he said, with a
wink. That would be the work of a seventy-year-old set painter he just
signed on, based in Ostia.*

*This was all very risky work for Vidler's to engage in. For those who
knew what Harry was about and knew for whom I worked, for us to be
seen in public together would be enough of a scandal – and there were
quite a few clients of Connie's in Rome who were capable of leaping to
those conclusions. I could never even tell my father, years later, that I
had known Harry. He would have never forgiven me because I was not
only jeopardizing my own career but his, and our family name as well.*

*But it was not my own recklessness that compelled me to meet Harry on
his terms. I also could never tell my father – or anyone else for that matter, I
was sworn to secrecy – that I was following orders from Connie himself.
Just a month earlier he had come to the Rome offices, where he had called
me in and shut the door for a talk. I had sensed that Vidler's was not
doing well. These were still the worst years for the firm: first the Depres-
sion, then the war. I presumed he was about to fire me. My sales and
acquisitions were pitiful enough; it would have been justified. Connie
had other plans for me, though. He had sized me up and realized I was
just ambitious enough, with a bent for duplicity and an overweening
desire to win the approval of those with the status both my father and
I aspired to, that I would not only comply with his directive to seek out*

fakes for acquisition but I would do my very best to excel. He knew who to pay off to keep me working out of Rome. It was my job to make it worth the firm's while.

Was it any wonder that I would end up writing a work about a young Machiavelli?

It really didn't take much for me to justify my new sideline. As Connie put it to me later that night over a simple roast chicken ("Always order the simplest dish on the menu, that's how you can tell how good the chef is," he said) and a couple of bottles of Valpolicella back at his hotel, the practice of those "in our line" trading in both fakes and genuine work was as old as the Grand Tour. "From Byres and Jenkins right up to bloody Sotheby's, nobody's squeaky clean in this racket." Connie had a sense of history and he knew what he was talking about. I realized he played the role of the vulgarian businessman to his advantage. Now here he was, showing his real cards and offering me the promise of a flourishing career if I played mine carefully as well. I slowly got drunk with him that night and ended up promising him my undying loyalty, of course.

Over the years it was Maes's stable of painters who could supply convincing fakes that I, with the help of Antony Farrell, would come to depend upon. It was all this work that eventually led to a plan that pleased the Curia in the Vatican and advanced their interests.

3

The Frieze

PART II

An explanation of the fallen fortunes of the Medici family,
with an introduction to Jacopo Corvo. An account of the trial of this
criminal for hire.

But let's not leave Niccolo yet,
There's more of him that should be told.
What caused this playwright such regret
Was what remained unsaid when old,
Of how he could remember when
His father, among all the men
In town would cut a pleasing form
On streets and squares, where still the norm
Was what would pass as dandified
In capitals abroad, and grave
Solicitors knew to behave
As clerics, scornful of such pride,
Unswayed by the parade of vain
Young men entranced by worldly gain

Who, in Savonarola's eyes,
The priest whose fiery words seduced
The city fathers and unloosed
A reign of terror on the wise,

Because so many had the nerve
To live, not solely just to serve
But openly espouse a mode
Of elegance, to flout a code
Of joyless self-denial, and who
Looked to the ancients rather than
The saints to ask just what is man
And why the truths that we once knew
Of beauty, and of living well
Would now condemn a man to hell.

In any work of historical fiction it is instructive to look at what is based on record and what is pure invention. Yes, Machiavelli's father was a lawyer, a man who had a small library and knew his Greek and Roman authors. Yes, the family name and status within Florentine society had fallen considerably by the time Niccolo was born, but none of what I have written about here – a trial of this street thug named Corvo, a knife pulled outside of the courtroom – had ever happened to a Machiavelli in Florence.

You could call it a curious departure from fact. I don't want to psychologize all of this too much (Freud, let's be honest, was a good fiction writer and art critic, but that is the only value of his work.), yet it is in a broader outline of this figure of Machiavelli's father that I see some parallels with the story of my father Peter Kluge: a dandified self-made man who attains some prominence and respect in an ossified aristocracy, one where his superiors are fiercely clinging to their crumbling hold on power. He takes one step too far, does not realize he has jeopardized the interests of those who once found him useful and is publicly sacrificed and driven into a state of ignominious exile for the rest of his life. It is the son's duty to redeem his honour and status.

Our family never spoke of what finally drove my father to leave Russia. He always attributed the sudden decision to his wisdom and foresight, his ability to see his own fate in the carefully plotted revenge killings of those who put down the 1905 revolution, including oafs like Sipyagin and Von Plehve, his friends in Nicholas's cabinet. My father would have never admitted that he actually benefited from the reforms of the 1905 uprising. He fought proudly for the Czar in Sevastopol and had this unshakeable belief that he would have risen up through the ranks of his own accord. How fitting it was that he retreated into a trade in antiquities in exile and prided himself on his encyclopedic knowledge of the ancient world. It was all a safe distance from the present and its promise of relentless disillusionment.

It was also a safe distance from the London where he found himself far from an equal partner in my uncle Theodore's jewelry business, so that he leapt at the offer to work for Connie Vidler, who was taking an interest in the political ferment in Russia for its opportunities in plunder and needed someone who would be trusted to be his agent. That is how my father ended up spending the last thirty years of his life a citizen of Istanbul, with his one last candle of hope and idealism flickering for me as the Kluge(r) who would become truly English.

He made his money and his career for Connie in Turkey on what began as a fool's errand. Connie knew that there was a fortune in antiquities there, and that his German colleagues (read competitors) in the auction house racket, through their government's contract to provide Turkey with a railway and the new culture ministry's heritage initiative, had managed to plunder a great deal. He needed a kind of prospector who could insinuate himself among the collection of bureaucrats, archaeologists and con men so he could cut in on their take. My father had been useful gaining access to some paintings and objets d'art from his old contacts in St. Petersburg and Moscow, but he knew virtually no one in Istanbul. He had his shape-shifter's gifts for languages and manners, his confidence man's intelligence and his knack for survival. Perhaps he ended up a bitter man because his success condemned him to a kind of rootlessness befitting gutted ambitions.

Yet there may have been an incident I unconsciously dramatized by writing this scene about Niccolo's father in Ocular, *one that had everything to do with his work for Vidler's. You see my father was always vague about how he managed to get a fair amount of Russian art – and art owned by Russians – into London in those first years after he had settled us all in Kensington. There was this unspoken rule that the family hardly ever mixed with other Russians in London. If my father had wanted to settle us in a real community of exiles, the logic went, we would have moved to Berlin or Paris. Perhaps it was my mother's influence, but they desperately wanted to become more English than the English. They both just seemed to superimpose all their loyalties and beliefs in empire from one crumbling edifice on to another. I remember my mother once speaking of the Russians in London in her usual disparaging tone. She said there was a distinct type of bohemian failure that insinuated himself in most cultural gatherings. She called them underground men – and she loathed Dostoyevsky.*

Anyway, "the incident." I still think on it and wonder what it all meant. I must have been no older than ten or eleven, at that age when one is still put to bed early, only to find oneself staring up at the plaster patterns in the ceiling. I had listened to Katherine, our governess, finally sneak into the cabinet and pour a cognac before retiring for the night. Then there was the long stretch of darkness and the London night music, full of the street shouts, the old floorboards creaking in deep cello bowscrapes, the wind rattling the windowpanes in faint shudders until my parents would return. They bustled in, just barely keeping an argument to a whisper. They were speaking Russian so I knew it was serious; my mother had strictly enforced an English-only policy in the house. Still I could pick out enough remembered words to understand something happened involving one of these underground men characters. My father was downplaying its significance while my mother was insisting he talk to the police. She said he had a peasant's mistrust for the law and that this thug meant it when he declared my father was on his list. I am no doubt misremembering, filling in some details from what I later learned about Comintern in those days. Still I wonder. It wasn't too long after that my father left London for Istanbul, leaving my mother to raise Olivia and me all on her own for the next five years. Maybe he had reason to fear for his life as an unapologetic supporter of the White Guard.

I now read this whole incident with Corvo and the knife, the fall from honour and banishment of Niccolo's father, as the kind of lie that gave me license to transmute, then break apart the truth.

Niccolo's father played it close
Like one who's added up the cost
Of all that's gambled and who knows
A wise man vanquished hasn't lost.
For fortune's fleeting, say the wise,
Time tears its blade through each disguise
That mere ambition fashions for
The man who fears he has no core
Beliefs and knows that death's cold hand
Wants nothing found within the purse
But nimble as a rich man's nurse
Extracts the ultimate demand,
The prize of every work of art,
That pound of flesh: the noble heart.

His swagger wasn't born of pride
As much as self-belief yet struck
His foes as far too dignified.
His courtroom victories owed to luck,
They said, and once he met defeat
The niggling doubts then would accrete
And form the damning argument:
"This upstart really wasn't meant
To take his place among the few
Sage legislators of the past,
His reputation couldn't last
In time, each spirit seeks its true,
Unfortunately fixed degree –
There's no one who is truly free.'

His nemesis came in the form
Of one who mirrored him in his
Belief his life defied the norm
Of minor figures. He had this
Same strut when walking, the aloof
Unfettered air, that no reproof

Could penetrate to shake his pride:
A murder suspect who had lied
And bribed his way to infamy
In lower courts for petty crime
Where rarely would he serve the time –
A cause was found to set him free –
Yet murder was a Rubicon:
If proven guilty hope was gone.

No friends in higher places could
Arrange for his release from jail.
The charge would stick, for once, for good.
No secret source would pay the bail.
And so, the stakes were raised beyond
Where they had ever been. The bond
Between Jacopo Corvo and
The powerful cabal who'd stand
Behind him as he went to trial
Would serve him well, Corvo believed,
He'd walk free, once again relieved
No one could challenge his denial.
Niccolo's father paid no mind,
Convinced he'd win – he walked in blind.

For Corvo's guilt was ironclad,
And only some appeal to grace
Would save this hired thug: he had
His alibi unthreaded word
By word, exposed as an absurd
Attempt to shamelessly deceive,
His fate was sealed with no reprieve.
But on the final day in court
As Corvo's bailiffs led him through
The crowd, his blade came into view
With one pull from his boot, a short,
Sharp lunge towards his nemesis,

Stunned all – that he attempted this.

Before he really could react
Niccolo's father felt the blade.
He stumbled, more from the impact
The stab was publicly displayed.
The crowd began to move as one
To watch what Corvo had begun
Instead of overwhelming him.
The ladies watching, poised and prim
Had sensed a spectacle at hand
And shivered with the thrill of how
A trial so tedious was now
A street fight, raw, and man to man.
When Corvo was at last subdued
This coda would at once occlude

The trial and serve to trivialize
The silent moves of those behind
This hired thug, the veil of lies
Niccolo's father knew defined
How power must present itself
To shroud the subtle ways that wealth
And influence could still remain
Within this state the sole domain
Of families that over time
Had seized the levers of control
Of church and state. They owned each soul,
Dictated what was deemed a crime.
As stars within the firmament
Each fate was fixed and permanent.

The fixers in this case were those
Led by the Cardinal, who could
Ensure this chapter would soon close
By stating that a mistrial would

Have to be called. This contretemps
Lulled justice to a state becalmed
And while Niccolo's father healed,
What he convincingly revealed
Res publica would soon forget.
His eminence Della Rovere –
Who laid these machinations bare
To save the crow that was his pet –
Would choose a prosecutor who
Could throw the case, protect the few.

And once Niccolo's father felt
That he was ready to return
To practice, all his cards were dealt,
He'd folded. He was soon to learn,
No case of import came his way;
No jury would be his to sway
On what could once compel or claim
A measure of his former fame.
For all his keen intelligence
He failed to see the grand design,
Believed in punishment condign,
A victim of his innocence
Whose fate had pierced Niccolo's heart,
And shaped what would become his art.

The Frieze

PART III

*An introduction to Andalus, apprentice to Leonardo in Milan, with
a short discourse on painting in the form of a dialogue.*

Now just a few years older than
Niccolo was a painter who
Had come to Florence, a young man
Among the enterprising few
Seduced by word that here amid
The studios a genius hid,
Who rarely painted. Such were the
Demands his patrons made that he
Could never concentrate for long
Without requests for some design
That called upon his eye for line
And form, his wit for word and song
To mount some entertainment or
To sketch an engine made for war.

He could resolve to put his mind
And palette to the mystery
Of all that is revealed, defined
Upon a work's trajectory
From deep within that fumbling state

Where every artist feels the weight
Of all that's been attempted by
The painters he cannot deny
As influences, while he still
Attempts to visualize anew
An image that he knows is true
And formed beyond what he could will
From such attainment of technique.
But muses whisper, never speak.

Long before I had received the postcard from the son of Ranuccio Tomassoni, I had often reflected on how much of him made his way into the character of Andalus.

Andalus, like Machiavelli's father, is an invention. Niccolo's education may drive the plot but it is the education of Andalus that provides the counterpoint. One is schooled in the art of politics and the other in the politics of art, yet both come to understand the power of seduction and its power to shape – or destroy – lives.

Ranuccio was a curious, one-of-a-kind discovery among the forgers Harry worked with. He came out of that poor, religiously conservative world that was oblivious to what was happening in painting at the time. He had taught himself everything he knew by simply looking at paintings and then reading everything he could find about what the artists had said or written about their own techniques. Such an approach made for excellent forgeries, but, despite my own belief in his talent, I knew that his original work would be greeted with silence, if not ridicule, by the critical establishment should he have even gotten a show in London or Paris.

And of course I also realize, as I re-read this novella, already anachronistic, why I still think on him so much. We are alike in this sense, mining a vein long abandoned.

The few paintings that were exhibited, including the three I purchased, remind me of the Borges story "Pierre Menard, Author of the Quixote," *where the main character rewrites Cervantes word for word. And yet the simple fact that he has conjured them through his consciousness makes him a master of a new technique of "deliberate anachronism" and "erroneous attribution."*

Anachronism was essential for Harry Maes – and Connie Vidler too. The bigger auction houses had gotten a lot more sophisticated during the thirties and forties with their methods of detecting fakes, and that meant a painter like Tomassoni had to do his research to figure out how the Renaissance painters created the texture of their brushstrokes and the colours of their palette. He had to work like an alchemist with everything from eggshells to horsehair to cinders to come up with the required effects. The steady industry of aping the style of work attributed to Cimabue, to Giotto and yes, even to da Vinci, naturally had its effect on Tomassoni's approach to portraiture and to perspective.

The more I got to know Tomassoni, the more I felt he was not really capable of forgery. He had to believe in every stroke he put on the canvas. Like an anthropologist who goes up the Amazon to live with a tribe and then "goes native" to such a degree he cannot remember his former identity, Tomassoni had wandered up the river that was the past and could not find an artistic route back to the present.

He was a provincial. He was not of the world that Harry Maes or Antony Farrell knew and worked within. His mother had taken him out of school at thirteen because he had to bring money into the house, and that meant doing everything from washing dishes to learning to cook in his uncle's tavern. Yet he fascinated me. What he established as first principles for his art came from his obsessive sketching and from what inspired him, wandering like a pilgrim through Rome to find the paintings that moved him. He had his pantheon of painter gods he went to again and again. They had perfected all he hoped to accomplish, and there was ample evidence at the time to suggest any contemporary art or culture had been reduced to a kind of signaling through the flames. The vanities, the bonfire and all that: Savonarola meant more to him than any arch-modernist like a Clement Greenberg ever could.

These muses summon, when all's clear
To serve them when they're close at hand
Without a second guess for fear

The patron will not understand.
This creed was all Andalus could
Attest as knowledge when he stood
Before this Leonardo in
His studio, where to begin
An explanation as to why
He thought as an apprentice he
Could claim, in time, some mastery.
He couldn't look him in the eye.
Took all he had to say his piece.
Now what he hoped for was release

From any expectation that
His journeyman's conceptions were
A tune that hadn't fallen flat.
Such miracles perhaps occur.
But what he met with from his host
Was silence of a kind that most
Apprentices would take to mean
His words revealed a philistine
Conception of the painter's art.
Yet then, much to his mute surprise
Light played in Leonardo's eyes.
A smile betrayed his softened heart.
He gestured to an empty chair,
Then laughed, shook off his sombre air.

"I don't agree with anything
You say about these muses who
Will shape what I'm intuiting …
Do you, in faith, believe that's true?"
Yet as Andalus tried to speak
One look caused him to play the meek
Believer turned to acolyte
In thrall, as he is shown the light
Perhaps imagining that here,

Despite this self-perfected pose,
His master could be one of those
Made vulnerable just by the mere
Suggestion that his solitude
Was transient as a passing mood

And that, if now as mentor to
This boy, a crack of light came in
To colour what of him was true
Beyond the innocence of sin.
"To paint is simply to inquire
With elements of earth and fire
And air, transmuted and infused
To form the palette that is used,
Within the alchemy of form,
To dramatize the way we see
In moments of epiphany
Just like that flash before a storm,
When something deeper is revealed
Than light and shade will crudely yield."

The confidence with which this was
Declared, as if no sense of doubt
Remained, that fundamental laws
Had been defined and all worked out
As if a problem had been solved
Seemed to discount the work involved.
The battle raged between the hand
That struggles with the work's demands
And what the mind envisions from
The start, Andalus realized.
Such trials, in Leonardo's eyes,
Were elegantly overcome.
So either he was touched by God
Or just a very clever fraud.

Maybe it's just a bad joke of fate that the English rhyme God with fraud.
All acts of imagination are touched with fakery and deception, aren't they?
Some more than others. I am speaking of the limitations of my own work
here and my belief I would not have to be the insufferable poseur with his
thesaurus in his back pocket for the rest of my life when I wrote this.

    The one who did manage to transcend the status of a poseur and out-
sider was my sister Olivia. Five years younger than me, she had no
memory of Russia at all and grew up on the English of the radio and
the movies. She had my father's wavy black hair and black eyes too,
which won her the Spanish gypsy role of Donalinda in a musical at
Kensit Hall grammar school called Andalusian Airs *– a musical that*
was as horrible as it sounds. By the time Vidler's found me a place in
appraisals in the Roman office, Olivia was at the RSC and was moving
in the circles of all my old classmates. She was loved by all of the young
playwrights and composers I once knew; she wasn't a threat to them.

    This was as it should have been. She was lovable and charming, quite
a budding comedienne until the late forties. We were very close until
I went to Rome. Through the war years we both tried our very best
to correspond as often as possible. I loved her innocence, her optimism,
her love of Shakespeare and all she was discovering. She even wrote to
me of her early love affairs, and, as I said, all that affected how I made
Maddalena fall for Andalus (including the name of the character as a
nod to her first big role).

    But once I returned to London, Olivia and I grew distant over time,
which I attribute to the influence of her boyfriend, Martin O'Reilly.
Failed playwright, mediocre producer of radio dramas – now there was
a poseur and fake if there ever was one. Perhaps he was charismatic
when he was in his prime. It is true, in the photos of the two of them
he looks like a young Marlon Brando, with his black Irish intensity,
his bricklayer's build (his first trade and the one line of work where he
showed some talent). She told me she had auditioned for a play of his
that a company in the West End was giving a go and it was love at
first sight. But I was not the only one who found Martin O'Reilly an
alcoholic boor with a chip on his shoulder. Her friends also noticed the
change in her, how he had made her feel guilty for her love of the RSC,

told her that her comedic talents made her nothing but a trained seal for the ruling class. She became sullen, cowed, humourless. I tried to tell her what I thought but there was really nothing I could say. There is that term made famous in the seventies for those hostages who come to love their captors – the Stockholm syndrome. That is what seemed to happen to her for the two decades she was with, but never married to, O'Reilly.

She did not have very many positive things to say about Ocular Proof *when I first gave it to her, chapter by chapter, through the dingy, grey, canned-beans-and-cheap-shoes years '46 to '48. I suspected she was just repeating what O'Reilly told her when she said it was work that betrayed my aspirations to gain the approval of the crypto-fascists who had almost handed Britain over to Hitler.*

About four or five years ago, when she summered here with me, she wept and apologized for all that, one night over too much wine. Yet despite all the many things that O'Reilly was wrong about, perhaps he wasn't quite off the mark there.

"As but a cursory knowledge of
The past affirms is still the case,
As harsh as unrequited love
And just as easy to erase
From what the simple heart maintains
As etched in blood, in fact remains
A memory for those who paid
The painter and for whom he made
The work – his secret pantheon –
For even they, within one life
Will prove less constant than a wife,
So all you can rely upon
In art is what eludes each youth:
The moment of a deeper truth.

"If thinking through each work this way
Does not compel you to retract
Into what currently holds sway,

Where art is just another act
In courts where one must still amuse
And never challenge or confuse.
If you can have the courage to
Believe that painting can be true
To what's, in sum, a nobler aim,
Then maybe what has brought you here
Is more profound than what I fear.
I couldn't care from where you came,
Because I'm sure I came from less
And art's a poor form of redress."

Andalus, like a pilgrim, bowed
His head, and let the words descend
From head to heart, words he would vow
To not betray until his end.
To cavil with this argument
Was ill advised, best to relent
And show that he could recognize
The comforts of consoling lies
A lesser artist tells himself
To turn from the uncertainty
Of just this stoic dignity
Required to scoff at fame and wealth
And trust the ice that pricks the heart
And unconsoled, turns dross to art.

The Frieze

PART IV

An introduction to the portrait that shapes the destiny of Andalus and Maddalena, daughter of Lorenzo de Medici, with some words on the education of her heart.

The sole work of this painter that
Bears mention here remains the one
For which this Maddalena sat:
A portrait thought destroyed, that none
Of the historians of the age
Had more than mentioned on a page
Of works that Leonardo had
Begun, when like a lost nomad
He'd been cast out of Florence to
Seek patronage in cities, towns
That had a sense of his renown
In any art he would pursue
As architect or painter or
As engineer – ambition's whore.

Ambition, and perhaps his own
Inquisitive impulse to learn
The essence of each art and hone
What nature and his quiet, stern

Approach to thinking through, or past
Received ideas, his will to cast
Off influences when they came
Between his vision and the frame
That limits and in time, defines
Each work as engine of desire
Had both seduced and yes, inspired
The one who traced each arc and line
Of his, this young man Andalus,
With too much talent, too much trust.

And eager to take on as much
As Leonardo would allow,
Which made this portrait project such
A clear inducement prized, and how
The mentor finally ceded to
The pupil underpainter, who
Through daily sittings for the work
Which Leonardo seemed to shirk
At every chance that he could find
To get back to what really claimed
His focus – that unknown, unnamed
Obsession he could not define
As anything he'd tried before –
Andalus claimed his place – and more.

How Maddalena claimed his heart
In turn the work hardly reveals.
The force of more than simply art
Is what her cryptic smile conceals,
And yet she barely was beyond
Her awkward teenage years, this bond
Of marriage she'd made to Cybo
Was all that she could claim to know
Of what a love was meant to be
And what she could expect of one

Who wooed her, told her there were none
Who could compare to her, that she
Was more than just her father's girl,
That two could make of love a world.

For she had lived behind the walls
Of well appointed prisons where
Within the cloistered courtyard halls
She'd find the garden, take the air
While tutored by the greatest minds
That il Magnifico could find
Among the broken poets who
Marsilio Ficino drew
Within his influence, he'd found
By forming his own school of thought
Where "lost" Hermetic texts were taught,
A willing patron to propound
The dangerous beliefs of those
Who shaped the order of the rose ...

Before such thought was crystallized
And wrapped in trappings of belief,
A totem of an organized
Resistance to the church as thief
Of all that spoke of mystery,
A deeper sense of history
That found in ancient texts the case
For transmutations of the base
To gold – so made a parable,
A code of secret rite that tried,
By how each soul is purified
To form a process comparable;
The alchemy that forms a true
Enduring heart so prized – so few.

Above is the first explicit mention of what I considered the secret history of da Vinci and his hermetic investigations. This would come to shape much of the theory behind The Camera and the Photograph: da Vinci's Shroud.

I suppose there are a number of reasons why I chose to focus on Leonardo's membership in a secret society, an idea which was, when I wrote this in the forties, just an amusing line of inquiry rather than a serious assertion.

From as far back as my Cambridge years, I had sought out membership in secret organizations as if I was seeking out appropriate models for living a double life. First there was the secret fraternity of Sebastian at Cambridge, then later of course, while working at Vidler's in Rome, my time with the Othello Project.

Working with MI6 appealed to me because so much of my upbringing as the son of Peter Kluge in London seemed an act of theatre. In public my family was a caricature of bourgeois English rectitude, while literally behind closed doors there were passionate arguments in Russian, a clash of my father's sad, neurotic denial of Jewishness and much shame about family with my mother's longing for life in Moscow, where her family name meant something. She was a character out of a Chekhov play; she harboured these delusional beliefs that she could return to a Russia that would mean her no harm and let her live as she had been raised, while my father had his own delusions of mobility and ambition rewarded in England. Even at the age of twelve I knew our horizons were limited, regardless of where I would be educated and what I would achieve.

I looked to my family and went through the typical rebellion much later than my friends. It was only at Cambridge that I condemned my father because he had willingly become another man's lackey. To me, Connie Vidler was this confidence man who instinctively knew how to exploit my father's weakness, and my mother and later my sister became sleepwalkers in permanent exile from a world that no longer existed, and willing accomplices in a public charade. The world Antony Farrell introduced me to in Rome was the only one that had any authenticity or true aesthetic value.

The Leonardo character in Ocular *is a Renaissance man in the same way his patron Lorenzo de Medici is; they have their private agendas and their public lives and an understanding of the dance with power that was required to serve their own ends. There will be people sacrificed along the way, people one might even presume they cared for, even loved, but to attribute such feelings to these men is like trying to make metal from quicksilver. I, too, painted from life.*

This sounded like a fairy tale
When Maddalena, as a child
Had first been tutored and regaled
With poems and songs as she had whiled
Away the summer days within
This garden where, she read, that sin
Emerged, a serpent in a bed
Of one's impatiens, and had led,
By whispering what the heart
Requires to truly feel alive,
And that resisting just deprives
Oneself of what the greatest art
Will by its nature celebrate
(Such fairy tales can bear this freight).

A child of too much time alone
To live in books and thoughts of love
She slowly came into her own
Sense of her beauty's power and of
The necessary artifice
Behind a furtive laugh or kiss,
And as the symbols in a poem
Or painting could be read and come
To turn what shocked and puzzled first
To intimations of a true,
Pure presence coursing, moving through
The work, she knew that she was cursed
To keep her heart protected by
A cool reserve, a living lie.

But only to ensure that when
She felt the love was real, she could
Bring this performance to an end,
Surrender to the highest good
The soul can ever work to sound
The depths of, in its most profound
Expression, and reveal her true
Self-portrait, limned from all she knew
Of how much light and shade within
Her came to shape her saddest smile,
And what would make her heart pound while
Andalus gently touched her skin
As if to find that perfect line
To justify his heart's designs.

For in their time together they
Transcended what they knew as fate
And Maddalena found a way
To see within her something great
And strong and pure – or so she said –
When questioning herself what led
To such a clear renouncing of
What she'd once defined as love
With all its expectations met
As passed on to her as a child
And likened to the way a wild
Bird of the woods became a pet,
She'd now resolve to be her own
Dark night bird who would fly alone.

This painting now was found among
A secret cache, revealed because
A noble family who had long
Exhausted all the wealth they had
Invested in this Nero's mad
Debacle of an empire led

By ignorant and overfed
Vulgarians and decadents
Who chose to plunder one of their
Old villas left within the care
Of this marchesa's supplicants
She gathered 'round her to proclaim
Her sordid bid for minor fame.

This is the sole moment in the work where I break the frame. Up until now, as in a play, it was possible to imagine my narrator in similar costume among the characters, yet here the actor stumbles over centuries, walks right off the stage and sits among those reading this work, speaking of a Marchesa who now owns this painting attributed to Andalus, and the "vulgarians and decadents" plundering a villa in the last days of Mussolini's "debacle." Then, like an iris effect in an old film, the image depicted closes to a pinpoint, the frieze concludes, and its characters are suddenly propelled into the story.

You could call this bold or simply dereliction of duty. You were supposed to line up your characters from the very beginning of a work and read them the riot act. "No larks," as Mr. Nabokov (or "that Mr. Sirin," as we called him) put it.

The truth is, there was a real Marchesa Vasi, and I was tasked, by Connie of course, to assess the value of the works of art within her estates, so when the time came for her and her hapless failed composer of a husband to go into exile in England they had enough money to take a kind of tenant's approach to citizenship and be left well enough alone. She did, as well, have a few paintings that could claim an impressive provenance, which entitled her to a degree of respect from an insufferable snob like me.

When my sister Olivia read this work back in London, she presumed I was speaking of the Marchesa Casati, that beautiful disaster Augustus John (whom Picasso nailed when he called him "the best bad painter in England") had fallen in love with. Olivia had come to know of the Marchesa later on in London, when she had become a destitute, deranged eccentric, wandering kohl-eyed through Knightsbridge with scavenged raven feathers in her hair. But I would have never been so

cruel to Casati; she was too worthy of my adulation then and now,
given her absolute, incorruptible commitment to making of herself and
her life a work of art, no matter what it cost her.

This breaking of the frame was just an aside directed towards Antony
Farrell, who knew how much I suffered completing the Vasi job.

And this Marchesa could recall
Once being told when she was young
That in her family's palace hall
The portrait had once proudly hung
Because through marriage long ago
Her family and the name Cybo
Had become intertwined, and what
Had lost its place within the glut
Of works of art the family owned,
(At one point catalogued as just
A minor work best kept in trust),
Its dark charms were what she alone,
In line with her eccentric tastes,
Had briefly loved then spurned in haste.

Now offered up for private sale
Among the last works she could find
To keep her from the debtors' jail,
Her pleas for clemency declined.
To make a case for it to be,
Appraised less for the filigree
That lines its oaken frame, is now
The way she'll save herself and how
She'll woo the constellation of
Defenders of the aesthete's creed,
Those touched with glamour once, who need
An undiscovered work to love,
A long forgotten painter who
Had genius (deemed by those who knew).

They gamely spread the word, to serve
To raise the portrait's price and give
Andalus what he might deserve:
What was denied him when he lived
Within the shadow of the man
Whose range of work within the span
Of just two decades changed the way
An image fixed in time could play
Upon the eyes, the heart and mind.
Andalus shared his master's fierce
Devotion to make beauty pierce
The veil of what was ill defined
And idealized, this portrait burns
To render how the true heart yearns.

Nigredo
PART I

*Niccolo's induction into the cabal of della Rovere through
the graces of his father's friend Jacopo Salviati. A brief explanation of
the roles he must play for two masters: Lorenzo de Medici
and Pope Innocent VIII.*

I had structured the plot around the four phases of the alchemical process:
nigredo, albedo, citrinitas, and rubedo. Nigredo represented the "blackening" of the prima materia; I wrote the scenes that proceed to suggest a
darkening of all of the elements of the plot that I had fashioned within
this "frieze."

I spent my days, probably because I had little else to do in those last
months of the war, jotting down what would come to be the structure of
this work. I was always a great believer in design. Sometimes I think
that if I had been born at a different time or place I would have been
some mediocre architect with an excessive enthusiasm for the baroque.
Or maybe something a little more modern and "eccentric" (the snob's
euphemism for crazy), like Gaudi.

Now I look back on all that and of course I think, what did it all
matter? This work was read by a handful of people and undoubtedly
always will be. And I am far too cynical and too much of an old Roman
to believe in posterity or some romantic notion of immortality. And yet I
know what I was intending to do by plotting it all out so carefully. This
was an act of love to the dead – all the writers and artists I had grown

up admiring. I wanted it to stand on its own, should I have never made it out of Italy alive.

The latter possibility was very real. I was corresponding with Kurt Malaparte in those last months – he had let me stay at his home on Capri, after I had left Rome – and through the American High Command I had heard reports of Russian soldiers in the outlying regions of Hitler's crumbling empire not just reclaiming territory but looting and pillaging, a dark, Chaplinesque parody of the sack of Rome.

And of course there was the more genteel pillaging being carried out by the Nazis of the paintings and antiquities throughout Italy that suggested, should Hitler's plans for the Reich be as real as reported, all this too would be sacrificed in the final days of this war. This was precisely what MI6 and the Vatican's Curia feared, and why Antony and I had been very busy working with painters like Tomassoni in the months before that spring.

All this mania to preserve something of "real" value. It was after the war, once I was living in London again, that I let my membership lapse with those in the authenticity racket. I came to the conclusion that fiction, like the writing of history itself, was most honest when it wore its artifice and unreliability proudly.

Some years had passed since the mistrial
That set Jacopo Corvo free
To walk the streets of Florence while
Niccolo's father quietly
Became a humble clerk and lost
What status he had claimed, the cost
Of once presuming that he could
Affirm a sense of higher good
Than justice as it was conferred
Upon those who could not rely
On wealth or power to defy
The ways in which the lines were blurred
In this, Medici's private state
Between the force of truth and fate …

Or destiny, as it was viewed
To weigh so heavily upon
Each soul as citizen imbued
With finite means to vault beyond
An order fixed by family name
That neither glory, wealth nor fame
Amassed through talents manifest
Or simply granted to those blessed
With beauty which, one could concede
Required its own intelligence
In order to beguile, convince
The ones who never felt the need
To educate the simple heart
And plunge into the depths of art

Which was, just like the oceans crossed
To find new routes to trade and gold,
Discovered to envelop lost
Empires' remains – untouched, untold.
As lines upon a map could not
Etch in the truths that Rome forgot
(Or found it wiser to conceal)
These hidden worlds could be revealed
Just solely through the process where
The stark *prima materia* of
The work – " as below, so above" –
From earth and water, fire and air
Were elements transmuted in
The art and in the soul within.

As below, so above … *This is just the first among a few variations
of a quotation that appears in the text, attributed to* The Emerald
Tablet of Hermes Trismegistus: "That which is Below corresponds
to that which is Above, and that which is Above, corresponds to
that which is Below, to accomplish the miracles of the One Thing."
It is the basic principle at work in alchemy and its transmutations, and

the Emerald Tablet was, as it was practiced in Europe, the primary source for these occult practices. Evoking the phrase was a kind of shib-boleth among the societies and orders that believed in alchemy not just as a viable process but also as a code of an alternative history, a secret faith. Yes, see MI6.

Yet such arcane discoveries
Were far beyond Niccolo's reach
And though he had the charm to please
He had no mentor who could teach
Him how to navigate his way
Through Florence and how to display
His usefulness to those in power,
Ensuring it would not devour
The subtle arts of governance
That kept in check the restive mob
And that it was a prince's job
To radiate beneficence
Regardless of what could be less
Than noble aims he might possess.

Niccolo's father knew that he
Would never get the chance to rise
Above to where his destiny
Fulfilled his sense of enterprise
Without one of his friends who still
Was well connected and could fill
The role of mentor for the boy,
A wise courtier who still enjoyed
The company of those who held
Positions where they pulled the strings
And knew which one of Dante's rings
Of hell the wisest traitors dwelled
And cast themselves in this image –
Or claimed a direct lineage.

There was one man best suited for
This: Jacopo Salviati,
Who moved among the rich, the poor,
The criminals, literati
With ease and with a cardsharp's eye
For where the power would really lie
Among the privileged and elect
Within the court and could direct
Niccolo through the perilous
Terrain of taverns, corridors
And palace halls where priests and whores,
The dull and once-thought-marvellous,
Had welcome smiles for innocence,
The pliant hearts one could convince

Or even, every now and then
Seduce, should fortune wear a smile
As well, and no one could defend
This new object of desire while
Among the threadbare pageantry
And calculated flattery
That ruled the dramaturgy of
The plots of power and courtly love
The logic of a subterfuge
That brought the Machiavelli name
Back to a kind of minor fame
As far as Paris, Rome or Bruges
Inspired Niccolo late at night
To plot and dream – and finally write.

This fixer Salviati knew
The circle of della Rovere
Who carefully chose a select few
To dine some miles from Florence where
Each came to share intelligence
On whom Niccolo dubbed the Prince:

Lorenzo, "il Magnifico" …
Who'd now become the willing foe
Of those suspected in the plot
That failed to murder him and claim
The city in another's name
Before the name Medici got
A foothold in the Holy See
Through grafting on the family tree.

Salviati actually existed, a Florentine who ended up marrying Lucrezia de Medici, the eldest daughter of Lorenzo. The marriage ensured Salviati's upward mobility and he never discussed his warm relations with della Rovere, who was doing his utmost to limit the powers of the Medicis, especially in Rome.

At an earlier stage of writing I wanted to give Salviati more of a role, model him on Harry Maes, given his duplicity, his subtle means of working with both ally and enemy for tactical and transactional advantage.

Then news of Harry's death came, and the more I learned of the circumstances, the more I came to see in his last years a certain recklessness no Machiavellian – even a minor one like Salviati – would possess.

At first there was some question as to whether the Nazis actually "disappeared" Harry. But of course they did, they had the most reason to; he had spent years providing some very powerful men within their ranks fake Poussins, fake Vermeers, fake Caravaggios. He even boasted about it within his circle of film and theatre friends who managed to thrive in occupied Europe. Those people knew him the best, knew he had never really stopped acting or staging theatrical productions. Most painters, even the ones cynical enough to profit from Harry's support and connections, could never really take to him because of his candour about his motives. He would pronounce upon his own vulgarity, say that everything about his life, including his relationships with women and men, came down to nothing more than transactions of one kind or another, and that there was a beauty and a clarity to living within such a pure, radical truth (well, radical for then).

I doubt he would be anyone's pariah among painters today. Yet he was actually far more valuable and then far more dangerous to MI6 than he would have ever been among the culturati of the Occupation.

Harry knew everybody that mattered for me, but more important, he understood the connections. He could see into my motives and he understood my weaknesses and my strengths. After that first meeting in the St. Regis in Rome, he rose from his barstool and offered me a Turkish cigarette from his nickel-plated case. When I smiled and nodded he laughed and said, "Young Nicholas Kluge, one day you'll have to stop living the life you think your father wants for you. You're going to realize your secrets are only dangerous to yourself. Well, they were until now." And then he walked out into the street with that sly grin on his face. I believe he had a clairvoyant sense about me.

An heir legitimate in deed
If not in name who could attain
Through force of will the power to lead
A band through unheld lands to gain
The love and faith – and fear – of those
Who could not know how to oppose
The means by which the papal nod
Transformed a thug to man of God
Just as the Cardinalate could take
Medici's son – not yet a man
And raise him, following a plan,
Up through their loyal ranks to make
The boy a worthy candidate
To one day lead a papal state.

This all enraged della Rovere
Though rarely did he seem upset.
As Cardinal he had the air
Of one who willingly would let
Such obvious designs on power
Take shape and slowly come to flower.

Yet underneath that calm veneer
He slowly plotted out a clear
Route for himself to claim the crown
In Rome, just as a crow can wheel
Through darkened forests that conceal
The quickest journey overground.
He worked upon a higher plane,
Aloof from all he stood to gain.

And though he feared he'd disappoint,
Niccolo to this villa came,
His will honed to a shining point
To pin upon his host his name
And speak in practised phrases of
His skills and his abiding love
And loyalty to Innocent
The Pope supreme, benevolent,
Now faced with the Medici threat
With il Magnifico's designs
Beyond his fiefdom's set confines,
Who had it in his sights to get
His son the prize of papacy,
Thus launching this conspiracy.

Yes, yet another to prevent
What seemed among the neighbour states
A tyrant's worrying ascent
That sundered all polite debates
About stability and peace
Or some agreed upon surcease
To any larger claim to land.
The matter urgently at hand
Was how to hold this prince in check
Through means covert that would provide
A measurement of the divide
There was between how clear, direct

And honest were Medici's claims
To noble diplomatic aims.

For Florence wed to Rome was less
A Pax Romana than a threat
To carefully approach, address
So that the peace prevailed, and yet
A counterweight in power and fame
Like della Rovere could reclaim
The Holy See, for all who knew
Lorenzo could envision few
Who could impede his family's rise;
Not Sforza ruling in Milan
Or Naples, with King Ferdinand
(Both feckless, if assured, allies)
Had world enough or time to plot
The war before the peace was fought.

Yet all of this was like a dim
Outline glimpsed in the first of dawn
Of borderlands unknown to him
Who'd come to play the willing pawn.
Niccolo was received and met
By Salviati, who then let
The boy into a darkened room
Where tapestries of scarlet gloom
Concealed the fading light of day
And where a kind of supper scene
Of rapt disciples, poised and keen
As della Rovere spoke, held sway,
Was playing out – a fresco come
To life, more resonant for some

Among these willing few who cast
Their sharpest glances at this boy
Who, though too late for this repast

Seemed more than ready to enjoy
The crumbs of wit and sage advice
That came with the admission price
Of something like servility
(or forced, performed humility
at least), enacted for the one
Who had convened them at this home.
All these clandestine sons of Rome
Had sensed that something had begun
And that this boy's arrival here
Was fortune's turn at wheel and gear.

The Cardinal, in one cold stare
Had sized him up from cap to boot
And gestured to an empty chair
Beside him, then said, "Our recruit
Here stands well recommended from
An unnamed friend, who bade him come
And prove his skills of reportage,
For what we need is espionage
To plot our steps well in advance
And no one would suspect this whelp
Brought in just as a way to help
A fallen family who by chance,
I'm told, the father tried to ground
That black winged bird we've kept around.

"For those who know of whom I speak
You will recall the episode,
But now there is no cause to seek
A further measure that would bode
Ill for this young man's prospects or
His family's welfare anymore.
So let this serve as proof to those
Whom we must sadly name as foes
That in this heart there does reside

A place for clemency within,
A recognition that the sin
Must be atoned by deeds allied
With ours, the cause that will unite
Our friends and foes alike to fight

"Both Caliphate and princeling who
Would falsely claim a right to rule.
And rest assured our path is true
To peace, and to prevent the cruel
And the corrupt in all their plans
To drive us to the barren lands
Of pagan rule, by iron yoke,
No matter how they try to cloak
Their machinations to conceal
That ultimately what they hope
For we'll resist: to see a Pope,
The shepherd of the commonweal
As caged as a prized infidel,
A broken world, a living hell."

The Cardinal was not without
A flare for the dramatic line.
He knew that he who does not shout
To make his case, who can combine
A gravity of purpose and
The appearance of an offhand
But devastating eloquence
Will have such powers to convince
That he can let the silence fill
The room, as all heads turned to see
This boy's reaction, and what he
Replied to claim his place and still
The skepticism rippling through
The room, how he'd convince these few

Who could decide his fate for years
To come, if not his family's claim
To some return to grace, his fears
That now the Machiavelli name
Would never once again attain
A measure of respect. The stain
Of pride and hubris was so deep,
His guilt would never let him sleep
A night without thoughts of regret
If his one chance to wipe things clean
Was squandered in this opening scene
Of his real life. He'd either let
The acts upon the stage that lay
Ahead for him be his to play

As the protagonist or he
Would be left in a minor role.
Revisions of the plot would be
Impossible, and who'd console
Him that his character deserved
A better fate? The fool who swerved
From fortune's sunlit path and chose
The brambled route because the foes
That he might face when in plain view
Instilled him with such quaking fear,
Would have to face regret as mere
Denial of cowardice, the true
Desserts of one who could not wrest
The prize from all the falsely blessed.

And so, with all this firmly cast
In mind, Niccolo, with a nod
Of due humility for past
Transgressions of a father flawed
By overweening virtue, let
The silence deepen as he set

His gaze upon della Rovere
Then boldly he took on the air
Of lightness that could strike a chord
So unexpected, yet so right,
For years he would recall this night
As when he learned, more than the word
So artfully employed. His smile
Suggested wisdom, strength, and guile.

What words he finally uttered were
Forgettable, something about
How honoured that he was …. The stir
Within the room, without a doubt
He felt, though. He had claimed his place
Because no one could read his face
For vulnerabilities exposed,
His thoughts were like a tome still closed
Among the fluttering pages of
The entertainments, simple tales
A young man frequently regales
His elders with to win their love.
He seemed possessed of some mystique –
The source of which he could not speak.

And this impressed della Rovere
Enough for him to give the nod
To Salviati sitting there
In meek attendance, over-awed
By all that had transpired, but who
Knew well enough his master to
Discreetly summon those who cleared
The table, and to wipe his beard,
Suggesting now the time had come
To rise and call things to a close.
All idle talk of friends and foes
Alike would cease. All would be mum

At risk of death should any word
Be leaked of what had just occurred.

Niccolo rose and tried to keep
His eyes downcast, to look the part
Of one discreet, who could have deep
Reserves of strength, a noble heart
Should he be tested, but behind
The mask thoughts raced around his mind
Of how he could perform and show
Them all his worth, that he had no
Self-doubt or worse, the nagging thought
That far from any starring role
He'd given up his very soul
To serve some creaking hackneyed plot
Now launched into its opening scenes,
Unsure what all of it would mean.

The two men working in the Curia that we knew, Barney Quigley and "the leper" Delegarde, really didn't believe Antony and me when we spoke of Tomassoni's talents, so I remember we had resolved one night, after a dinner I still can taste because of the real bread and truffles (these old bastards always ate well in the Vatican apartments), to take them to the garage where Tomassoni was working, so they could see for themselves how talented he was.

It was early the next morning, in the middle of a heat wave in Rome, when we set out for Esquilino, where Tomassoni's uncle and aunt had their tavern near the Piazza Vittoria. The only time Ranuccio could get his painting in was either late at night or early in the morning, and Quigley ruled out late nights because he said all the war made him want to do was sleep. We downed too much espresso near the termini station and walked to that garage in the thick haze of dawn.

When we arrived, Ranuccio looked up and nodded in our direction. He was focused on the fold of a red robe within the portrait he was forging – Titian's Entombment. I introduced him to Quigley and Delegarde who seemed cowed and obsequious once they had had a chance to look at the work under the light of a welding lantern Tomassoni said he "found."

"So these are my real masters, yes?" he murmured to Antony, in that Calabrian dialect no one else but Farrell among us could decipher beyond the simplest phrases. He had stripped down to a pair of black football shorts, flecked in red paint, and he had a kerchief, soaked from a bucket of cool, filthy Tiber water, tied around his neck. "Why do I feel that I'll never really be free of you people?"

Perhaps it would have been better for him, in the end, if what he feared had actually come true.

7
Nigredo
PART II

The dialogue between Lorenzo and Innocent on the threats
of subversion, and the uses of art versus the uses of the object of faith.

Some weeks had passed, and in this time
Niccolo found himself, by way
Of letter sent, upon his climb
Far up the misty path that lay
Ahead for him, assigned alone
To serve Lorenzo, sent as Rome's
Amanuensis to the Prince.
The missive from the Pope convinced
His master that this "wise young man
Possessed of skills beyond his age
Will help us both. He'll assuage
Our fears that though my aged hand
Cannot be clasped in yours, this boy
Holds Papal trust in your employ.

"Just as your son's ascent
Within the Cardinalate claims
Some holy purchase and intent
For the revered Medici name
To some day take its place within

The Papal line, let us begin
To see our destinies entwined,
Two constellations now aligned
Through nuptials and a common cause
Inspired by wise St. Augustine
To work within our humble means
Affirmed in Papal bulls and laws
The sacred trust of government,
To set aright the firmament."

And this required some time to plan
A chance for both to steal away,
Assess each state down to the man
Who ruled: those likely to betray
And those with whom they still could trust,
How to appear as wise and just
In every move they made to both
Their subjects and to those whom, loath
To grant them any more than what
A fragile treaty would allow,
Were still constrained by deed and vow
From subterfuge and counterplot
To bonds thought prudent to adhere,
If not from love, then measured fear.

So in his palace, locked within
The library, where he would go
On many nights, where to begin
To scribble (reaching far below
His conscious thoughts for sudden bursts
Of music in the state he cursed
As reason's barren plain, where dreams
No longer flowed in quiet streams
To nurture flowering eloquence),
Seemed easier than letting sleep
Erase the mounting doubts he'd keep

Within himself. He'd now convince
This Pope he was an open book,
Read clearly with a cursory look.

"So glad that we at last can sit
As just two fathers in this home
All talk of money grinds my wit
To counterfeit, best coined in Rome,"
Said Innocent, with lupine grin
Revealed like a remembered sin,
"And all of that I'd rather leave
To Franceschetto, who believes
He's somehow won my trust because
Indulgences that he can grant
To every whining sycophant
Have vaulted him above the laws
We both through wisdom still adhere
To, knowing that the peril's clear.

"When one is seen to be unbound
By principle and virtues which
Your subjects still believe can stitch
The common thread to what is found
Within the rosary they cling
To, and in all the hymns they sing
As one, the music of their fears
In misalignment with the spheres
Yet gamely all notes must be hit.
The fluttering passion in each voice
Is what we have but little choice
To answer to, without remit,
And any sense that one has strayed
From holy writ is faith betrayed."

The conversation that follows between Pope Innocent VIII and Lorenzo is the basis for all the action that proceeds. The transaction that is established here – a counterfeit work that would inspire devotion among the masses in exchange for the Medici line positioning itself for the papacy and control of the Curia, was not just a bit of imaginative invention for me; I still believe it occurred. I was emboldened by some of the research Farrell had done into the camera obscura and the alchemical processes that would be used for the creation of paint pigments. I believed that Leonardo's studio really was a laboratory that Innocent would have done well to shut down. Lorenzo sanctioned and supported da Vinci's work from the very beginning out of a kind of neo-Platonic fraternal bond they established through their interest in the same pagan writers, the same courtier intellectuals led by Pico della Mirandola.

It's embarrassing to recall, but I had written Olivia an earnest declaration of my political intentions for the work. I told her that what I had hoped to do with this material was similar to what Brecht accomplished with his play about Galileo – present Leonardo as a "rationalist ahead of his time." The opposition he faces from the power structure was the same kind of opposition a true Marxist faced. At the root of all my earnest – but, thank God, brief – embrace of Marxist Leninism was a sense of faith just as powerful as that of anyone who still considered himself religious. And I'm sure I had a wish to maintain a connection to Olivia, after she had fallen in with O'Reilly.

However, this embarrassing earnestness was not the reason I stowed this draft away for decades. I have no shame about my former political beliefs. The world had changed, and it would have been unnatural if I hadn't changed as well. After a decade back in London after the war, I simply had no ambition or expectation of being discovered and enjoyed by any reader outside a small circle of friends.

As for my moving away from the left, the sixties had the most to do with it. As soon as virtually every young person became familiar with the thoughts and writings of such figures as Trotsky and Guevara, to pretend I was still the man I'd been in 1946 was to be a quaint and harmless anachronism, too old and too mixed up with "the establishment" to enjoy the comforts of credibility. And legitimacy, never mind

*the luxuries of being seen as an original figure, had always meant a
great deal to me.*

*I never felt I had the proof, so to speak, for what I believed were the
true origins of the Shroud of Turin. The proposition that I outline here
is an odd source to power a plot through scene after scene, one that began
with a conversation Antony and I had in Rome. I was convinced the
shroud was simply the first photograph, yet I knew what a provoca-
tion this would be to the Church and was not yet prepared to defend
myself in public over it. Books, like paintings, still mattered to the
Vatican as much as objects of faith, and the lightness of a casual
conversation between Antony and me was the proper context for these
speculations.*

Lorenzo smiled to mask his sense
That Innocent was sounding him
For some articulate defense
They both could summon. With a prim
And pious nod, he played his role
As if some god of mischief stole
The greater portion of his wit
And leapt inside a book to sit
And wait until the guest was gone
Among the many better selves
That whispered histories from the shelves
And left the prince to soldier on
As if now deafened to their words,
Compelled by what his fate conferred.

Upon him rested such a task
Of careful, measured compromise
He checked himself before he asked
What rankled him. "What wicked lies
About my governance has caused
You such concern? My many flaws
And failings I'll in faith concede,
But faith itself? No one could read

What I have said about this state
And its allegiance to the Pope
And question how I've mapped the scope
Of powers or how your rule dictates
The course of every crucial turn
In policy or state concern."

"And yet the rumours still persist,
It seems," said Innocent, "and I,
When probing deeper can't resist
To ask myself the question why
Pico della Mirandola
Arrives in Rome with but one goal: a
Page of questions for debate
He surely knows would instigate
A full blown insurrection of
The Cardinalate if they took
His premises as fact, forsook
An iron fist for silken glove,
Allowed the heresy he spouts
To license all discord and doubt.

"When you and I are both aware
How tenuous this current state
Of peace remains, I think it's fair
To ask why such an apostate
Would find an audience and home
In Florence to appeal to Rome
For audiences with the few
Within my court I trust. And through
It all, not once did you exert
The power and influence you claim
To halt him in his quest for fame
And credibility. He skirts
The censure of a patron who
Could rein him in: that would be you."

Lorenzo could not help but show
His obvious distaste when he
Took note of how a roseate glow
Now filled those sallow cheeks. To see
This petty tyrant stab the air
With crooked finger and his glare
Of sudden, unchecked rage was just
Enough for fraying bonds of trust
Between them to be snapped – and yet
They both had far too much to lose
Apart. Both knew that one can't choose
With whom one's best allied to set
A course where risk is minimized
And one's ambition realized.

So gamely he provided cause
For Innocent to feel that he
Had eyes to spot the troubling flaws
Within this House of Medici.
"Was not the work deemed harmless when
Your scholars had the chance to spend
Sufficient time to read it through
As treatise? An argued view –
No less, but certainly no more –
Is all that this compendium
Of theses, nine hundred in sum,
Should seriously be taken for.
A Vatican secure within
Does not view inquiry as sin."

"This harmless tome that you refer
To hardly points to just one man
There's quite a group – from which you were
Of mention as the guiding hand.
Now why would an academy
Be called 'Platonic?' Humour me

By offering a rationale
For pagan thought in this cabal
That's found great purchase in your court.
You know I've given you my trust
To frame our common cause as just.
A love for gaming, whores, and sport,
In truth, I'd rather you be known
For than a school I can't condone."

Lorenzo checked himself before
He let his temper fire the words
He tried to keep cold at their core.
For wise is he who always girds
Himself for battle with a friend
Who seeks one outcome in the end:
His own objective, shaped to look
As if two old friends both partook
In how the plan had found a form.
Agreements, like revenge, are best
Conceived as coldly as the jest
That seems as if it's just a warm
Acknowledgement of battles waged
When youth excused the force of rage.

"I ask you, would you not agree
That if I were to make of all
This esoteric inquiry
Dark heresy, would not the thrall
It held for those not quite as wise
Nor faithful as this group, comprised
Of those I'd call my closest friends,
Be much more dangerous in the end?
The knowledge that's forbidden fruit
Tastes sweeter, so the scriptures say,
Unless it's meant some other way
It seems impious to refute.

The boldest, brightest minds should not
Be heroes for a traitor's plot."

The smile of Innocent revealed
The blackened teeth and purple tongue
Of one who felt compelled to yield
To vices best left for the young.
"The problem, that you're not aware
Of, clearly, is what's in the air
In city states not quite as blessed
By placement on the map. The test
Of leadership, as far as I'm
Concerned, is whether one can see
The larger frame, our history –
The arduous and fitful climb
Out of the depths of pagan rule
Where servitude's a tyrant's school.

"The Caliphate is not the sole
Obsession of my sleepless nights.
Whole villages, where every soul
Is steeped in ancient, godless rites
Comprise a kind of Domesday book
Of failed conversion, long forsook
To superstition, household gods,
Alchemists, witches, traveling frauds
Who claim they have the power to heal
With relics from the holy lands
That somehow came into their hands
On pilgrimages to the real
Necropolis of old crusades
Where John had preached and Christ had prayed.

"You know yourself the power this wields.
The relics that we have attained
Can still attract, from far afield

The pilgrims who, with eyes untrained,
Perhaps, or souls unhinged enough
To find belief in such a rough
And threadbare rendering of the face
Of Jesus, daubed with all the grace
That one would more expect from those'
Apprenticing to one of your
Commissioned lapdogs you keep for
The pleasures from their studios
Than any image one could claim
With seriousness, in holy name.

"Yet I have had to study well
From stark necessity, the ways
My predecessors found to sell
Indulgences that served to raise
The treasury, for I'm sure you know
That currently the funds are so
Diminished that your son-in-law
Has done more in these months to claw
The Holy See out from the pit
Of certain bankruptcy. The dirt
Beneath his nails has helped us skirt
The fate of far worse hypocrites.
It's all caused me to realize
On what our claim to power relies.

"You have the bankers on your side
And they have served you well to make
A city-state well fortified
Where few have felt the tax you take
And anyone with any claim
To wealth recalls the fools who gamed
By plotting their conspiracy.
With admirable efficiency
Their executions carried out

Restored the sense of order and
Displayed you firmly in command.
No Florentine had any doubt
You knew it's better to be feared
Than loved. And that is why I'm here."

"You flatter me," Lorenzo said,
"Impute more wisdom than I'm due,
So many men have wished me dead
I'm lucky to be still with you."
He raised his glass of wine to toast
His honoured guest, to play the host
And fall into this pantomime
Of fulsome courtly praise, put rhyme
And flow back into what had veered
Into an obvious overture
Where Innocent hoped to secure
More than his trust, that much was clear.
Like so much else of his design
Not much could pass as genuine.

"The knives are drawn for me as well,
My friend. Ambition is the spur
That drives good men on into hell.
Who knows what is yet to occur?
And I am bound within my role
To wait like Charon for the toll
My precious cargo deems it fit
To pay me for the benefit
Of passage safe to what's beyond,
Yet this is no way to accrue
A fraction of the wealth that you
Can confidently draw upon:
To proffer wonder with a deft
Deployment's all that I have left."

When I think of my own ambition at this time, I wonder what I was really hoping for from my work at Vidler's, from all that I agreed to do for MI6. I had no interest in returning to London when the war ended. I did not want to have that conversation with my mother and father about why my relationship with Isabella Nadler, the Swiss Ambassador's daughter working at the Banco di Roma, had ended (her serial infidelities, not mine). I mulled over going to work for MI6; Farrell had said that was always an option for us both after the war. There was only one thing clear to me; I did not want to become Connie Vidler's lackey, like my father.

All I remember wanting for myself was to be in the background, to offer counsel and useful information when it was needed, to indulge my own appetites as discreetly as possible and to take notes. I was getting it all down for stories I believed I would one day have the courage to write. I suppose I really did see myself as a young Niccolo. I believe I existed in a world of extremes, between those with too much money and power and those, like Tomassoni, with none.

But of course I never really did summon up the courage to write imaginatively beyond this work, and even then, this story was a means of escapism for me. There were too many people whose careers and reputations I did not want to compromise – my father's especially. At a deeper level I never really got over my own sense of shame about why my life hadn't added up to more by then.

And yes, I made a life and a career of being in the background. I'm sure I became a puzzle to many, but that was a small price to pay for not having to risk damaging others' lives with the truth.

Yet even as careful and cautious as I was, someone was sacrificed, as Ranuccio Tomassoni's son knows only all too well now, it seems.

"And so, what I must now request
Of you, with all your ties to those
Who ply their arts, who you invest
In, for the truth that beauty knows
And oftentimes, with faith, reveals,
Is something with the look and feel
Of radiance that has left its mark

With such a presence that a stark
Impression of the man who walked
Among us as the son of God
Is captured, so that all the flawed
Attempts at relics that we've talked
About will be forgotten, and
My rule can take a firmer hand.

"We'll be assured of greater reach
And power to sway the pilgrims who
Will once again in faith beseech
Me for their souls to be renewed.
And as I grant, with payment made,
Indulgences, all fears allayed
For what awaits them when their rites
Are finally given, just the sight
Of some creation with the power
Some now-forgotten relics had
Will also, I assure you, pad
The mattress for your final hour,
For if we can't both benefit,
Pray, what would be the worth in it?"

With that, the Pope reached for the hand
Of Il Magnifico and held
It tightly for a moment and
Then smiled so warmly he dispelled
The sense of something like a threat
Lorenzo felt each time they met.
He knew this quip was more than just
Some random thought that with a gust
Of inspiration stirred the air
Within that room that suddenly
Seemed much too small. What possibly
Could be the one way he'd be spared
The vengeance of this hungry ghost
Required real art. That rankled most.

Nigredo

PART III

Andalus, accompanied by his own Virgil through the streets of Milan,
goes to meet Gethsemane, a woman with some knowledge of alchemy.
A dialogue on the true **Magnum Opus.**

Some distance from this quiet scene
The painter, Andalus, had come
To wander narrow streets, unseen
By those among the patrons from
The studio in Florence where
His master had decamped, the pair
Of them now working in Milan
To serve the court of the sole man
Whose power and wealth could one day prove
To rival il Magnifico:
Called "*il Moro,*" Ludovico
Sforza, who thought wise to remove
His family's rightful heirs to claim
The duchy, in both deed and name.

Yet Sforza barely mattered here,
Regarding what in Rome had just
Occurred, where one man's simmering fear
Of what he can't control or trust
Means that he must rely upon

A source that this Leviathan
Of power-as-faith or faith-in-power
Would rather crush before it flowered
Within some quiet garden of
Inquiry where the sole pursuit
Of knowledge yields the bitter fruit
Of truth – "as below, so above."
Andalus knew one woman who
Could prove the mystic's code as true.

And so to seek her out he set
His course within this labyrinthine
Redoubt of side streets he'd forget,
His bearings lost, without one sign
Upon a corner to return
Him to his starting point. He'd earn
At least an ounce of her respect
If in his eyes she could detect
The dogged innocence he'd need
To not just find her but to take
Her wisdom seriously and make
A true commitment to the creed
That solely through his father's name
He had some knowledge he could claim.

He found a tavern where the glow
From candles set about the room
Recalled what he had come to know
Of that austere monastic gloom
Within the Christian churches where
He'd gone in Leonardo's care
To learn the iconography
The ancient masters for a fee
Perhaps as measly as his pay
Had rendered, timeless and serene:
The stations, saints, the Nazarene

So vivid, as if yesterday
The gospel had been first revealed,
The fevered dream, the seventh seal.

These days I have been waking up with visions of my mother taking Olivia and me to the Russian Orthodox Church on Harvard Road. The smell of tallow, of old woolen coats and serge. The Bishop who seemed from the Middle Ages, his black eyes glaring out at sin made flesh and not forgiving a soul in the place.

In the early years our father wouldn't go, despite my mother telling him it would be good for him "for business prospects" to get to know the émigrés who went every week, to stand and weep like my mother, out of nostalgia more than any religiosity. He "could pass," she said.

It wasn't long after my father went to Istanbul that, curiously enough, my mother stopped going to church. Olivia believed it was because she had had an affair with Pavel Ionkin, a grim-faced man in grey flannel, eyes like a dead pig's, who was an actuary for Lloyd's of London. My mother had known him and his wife "back home." The possibility of my mother locking eyes with Yelena Ionkin, his wife, and having words with her was too real.

I had no idea. "Of course you didn't," Olivia said. "You were a boy, and boys do not pay attention to such things." I was not going to argue, even though in my mind I had always been the one who observed my mother the closest, in the hopes that I too might learn how to perform the role of someone nobler than I was. How could she hide it from me if she truly felt anything like love for some other man? I was no little Hamlet; that was clear.

But of course there are always things hidden, things you could never imagine about your parents. I should have put that down in a note to Ranuccio Tomassoni's son.

And with that, more on Andalus:

He'd found, perhaps from too much time
With Leonardo in the heat
Of inspiration, the moon's climb

Became the eye's celestial rhyme
For when these northerners attained
The height of honesty, the feigned
Familiarity of those
Who'd rather treat their friends as foes
(For profit was its own reward)
No longer had to grace the stage
Of public life. The quiet rage
The day exacted could be poured
As wine into the gambler's cup
Where broken men would come to sup.

So knowing that he'd be received
With circumspection here, at best,
He entered with what he believed
Could pass for just that self-possessed
Degree of humble rectitude
Required to quell the blackest mood
Of those who'd quickly take offence,
Or others who, at his expense
Would ridicule the courtly air
Of one who put himself above
Their station with the costume of
Some pampered fop, with perfumed hair,
And fingers ringed in golden bands
Too elegant for workman's hands.

He found himself a seat along
The table where the wine was poured
Then smiled at those nearby whose songs
Were those that couldn't be ignored.
They sang of dark-skinned concubines
" From where the sun so cruelly shines
Upon the heathen caliphate …"
And how these sirens sealed the fate
Of "many a seafaring fool,"

Then eyed him closely for a crack
In his composure, the attack
He'd launch in rage – or just the cool
Rejoinder that would then incite
The fatal urge to rise and fight.

Yet Andalus had years of such
Predictable attempts to goad
Him to react, there wasn't much
He hadn't heard, these episodes
Were best approached by sensing who
Among the less committed few
Seemed poised to slip away should there
Be so much tension in the air
You had to cut it with the blade
Andalus always kept for these
Occasions when one had to seize
The moment in these grim charades
That spoke of " murder scene begun;"
You singled out the weakest one.

And here it was an overfed
And greying actor that he'd seen
Perform in one of those unread
Old comedies put on between
Amusements at the Sforza court
Who seemed long wearied of the sport
In taverns where he could afford
The steady stream of wine they poured
Him, yet who couldn't quite assume
Within the confines of his role
Off-stage, the hint of noble soul
Who could transcend this sense of gloom
Of every place of refuge from
The fate he couldn't overcome.

Andalus finally caught his eye.
Once those who taunted him had seemed
To shake off both the how and why
He'd come to them, each ring that gleamed
Upon his finger wasn't worth
The struggle to extract. The dearth
Of any greater cause to kill
Him meant that he could drink his fill
As long as he did not but glance
In their direction, this he knew.
And so he counted out what few
Stray coins he had and took the chance
With glass in hand to move beside
The actor, awkward in his pride.

"You look to me as if you might
Know someone that I'm looking for;
Not that she'd be here at night
But I was told that through her door
Are welcome not just women who
Require her secrets, but a few
Wise gentlemen well schooled in thought
The Church would rather we forgot.
I'm speaking of these books I heard
She has, but under lock and key
She keeps them, just for those to see
Who comprehend what is conferred
Upon each soul who knows the real
Unvarnished work, and what's revealed."

"Untarnished might be what you mean
If you believe she'll bring you gold,"
The actor grinned. "I think you'd glean
As much from any bitter, old
Forgotten fraud with suspect 'cures'
As this Gethsemane of yours.

This sacred alchemy she claims
And honours with her chosen name
(She says it's where she found the book
That shaped her destiny and showed
Her, from the first pale stone that glowed
From transmutations that she took
Upon herself) is likely not
Much more than just her wishful thoughts."

Rather than this character, I initially wanted to give this name Gethsemane to the brothel in this scene, after the garden where Jesus and his disciples prayed the night before his crucifixion. Farrell, who read Ocular, *knew where I was going with this nod to the gospel, sanctuary, and prostitution, given what Pius was up to, yet I came to like the notion of this strong female figure, who was both pilgrim and alchemist, taking her name from the church near where she had come to find her books of Hermetic writings.*

And of course I wanted Olivia to see that by creating this character I was not quite the rich man's lapdog her boyfriend Martin O'Reilly thought I was. She told me he had scoffed at my reference to Brecht's Galileo *in a letter, said "the revolution does not need his kind" – seriously. Gethsemane was my attempt to show her that I was aware of an underground network that, like the Resistance, could count the older women in villages as some of its most effective operatives.*

Olivia never did tell me what she thought of this character – not even when she was in her sixties and had finally retired from acting with hardly more than her government pension and an NHS card to keep her in insulin. She seemed to have become a kind of Gethsemane character by then, long since celibate and almost reclusive with her holistic healing books that did little, if anything, for her diabetes. When she came to spend a summer with me I came very close to taking her in – she'd sold the family house to get out of debt – but I knew her pride would never allow it. She had to be the noble one, the martyr, while I grew into my role as the compromiser.

"But I can lead you, once I've downed
Your kindness here, to where she lives,
You wouldn't want to venture 'round
Here late at night, unless you'd give
Your life to meet her, and I trust
It's not for your designs you must
Involve yourself with such a crone.
I think you'd rather you were known
For work of nobler pedigree
Than what she calls the soul's true art
That purifies a darkened heart.
It's hardly worth the filigree
Within the frame of what you'd mount,
Your talent held to true account."

The actor's cynicism seemed
Well rooted in what he observed.
Andalus wondered if he'd schemed
At one time (and then lost the nerve)
To work in league with those like her
Who practised dark arts undeterred
By what would happen if revealed
To Cybo's forces far afield
From Rome's environs now, they said,
With mandate and resources to
Uncover and destroy the few
Real influences that had led
To tacit, if covert support
From those at the Medici court.

For many were the ones like him
Who, cursed with talents to amuse
And proud to claim they wrote a slim,
Unread but skilfully obtuse
Poetic testament of truths
Revealed when one still had his youth

And could still woo a simple heart
(Those years before he played the part
Of Aeneas, with Virgil's lines
Just barely rattling in the brain).
He still had hope he would attain
The sort of gravitas consigned
To holy fools and priests defrocked
That only philistines would mock.

They walked with just a lantern's light
To guide them through the quiet streets.
An actor with his catamite
Is how they looked. No fool would treat
Them any better or much worse
Than locals who within each purse
Had rarely more than pennies to
Provide to those that still were true
To codes that held for centuries
Regarding those deemed as a mark
And those left spared within the dark:
Who makes his name with skills to please
Or entertain, like whores, had earned
Safe passage 'til the dawn's return.

"The ladies I have taken here
Who found themselves in sudden need
Of treatment given that they feared
Months out of work, a mouth to feed –
A fear I shared, for truth be told
My pockets aren't quite lined with gold
From years devoted to the stage
And I'd be foolish at my age
To think my work could catch the eye
Of Sforza's or Medici's court.
My troupe of sirens still support
Me in the Spartan fashion I

Have always lived to ply my trade.
Their acting's where the money's made.

"They found Gethsemane to be,
For all her interest in arcane
Beliefs, the only one to free
Them from the painted woman's chains
Of motherhood, or ailments caused
By living by the ageless laws
That govern our desires and make
Of marriage vows the gambler's stake.
Gethsemane has medicines
And lost hermetic remedies
That heroes of my comedies
Rely on so their mortal sins
Don't claim for them a tragic fate:
Desire affirms what art dictates."

It wasn't clear to Andalus
From listening to the actor's tone
If he was actually serious
Or playing out what he was known
For when he strode upon the stage.
Perhaps it was, that at his age
The comic and the tragic had
Spun into one and so the mad
Declamatory stance was just
A way to ape the fool and spurn
The innocent, so that they'd learn
That there was no one you could trust
Except yourself. The only route
To art was through this absolute.

For he who claimed he'd found the path
To deeper truths would come to nought,
And that held for the polymath
As much as the apprentice brought

To kneel with solemn reverence
To those who said that ever since
The lost hermetic texts were found
At last there was the basis sound
Enough to crack the vessel fired
Within the walls of truths received
From Rome, where all that was believed
As sacred text the Vulgate's tired
And empty rhetoric affirmed,
With heretics denounced and burned.

These thoughts, like phantom forms in air
Andalus traced from memories
Of what his master chose to share
With him, embroiled in his unease
And tireless questioning of how
The painter's work could be endowed
With all the impact of the real,
So palpable that one could feel
The sense of time distilled, the trace
Of some mysterious light within
The image of desire, as in
The memory of a lover's face.
No method that denied such power
Could ever bring real art to flower.

And such a stark declarative
Within those final lines sufficed
To comfort him, this narrative
Would justify the sacrifice
And endless hours of work he'd give
To this pursuit. He'd rather live
And even risk his life like this
Out wandering at night with his
Old Virgil that would lead him on
Through purgatory's darkened streets,

Assured whoever they would meet
In secrecy, with curtains drawn,
Would bring him that much closer to
The pure, the genuine, the true.

"She's here." The actor smiled and raised
The lantern to an oaken door.
He knocked four times, then seemed unfazed
By who appeared, a painted whore
Who nodded, with the faintest grin
Then opened up and let them in.
"That witch does better business than
Us girls," she laughed, "though this young man
Should stick around here afterward."
She led them up the creaking stairs,
Just smiling for the startled glare
Of an old judge upon the third
Floor landing, as he scurried down,
A trail of shame in scarlet gown.

Then down the hall a curtain stirred.
A glint of golden light between
The folds allowed a glimpse, a word
That sounded like a curse. She'd seen
The two of them approaching and
Arose, reached out with wizened hand
To pull the curtain back, reveal
A room more like a cave, with sealed
And painted arches, meant to limn
A galaxy of glistening stars
With Phoebus in a tarnished car
Aloft, though with a visage grim
His gaze was fixed upon the guests,
Imperiously unimpressed.

"Gethsemane, this boy has come
For you, and judging by the way

He's dressed, I think he may have some
Resources that suggest he'd pay
As handsomely as he appears
For all the wisdom of your years,"
The actor with his courtly bow
Had caused the crone, with sunken brow
And gorgon's eyes of milky green
To take them in from head to toe,
Imagining what they might know,
The risks considered and foreseen
Of any truck with fops and fools
Entranced by thoughts of trade in jewels.

"Whatever wisdom I possess
Could hardly serve to stuff your purse
With bank notes, and as you might guess
I've seen your kind before – and worse –
Who've come, seduced by what they heard
Of alchemy, and undeterred
By how this Pope now classifies
Me as a witch, or how these lies
Could cause their own undoing, seem
To think that I could simply give
What is not learned but rather lived
As deeply as each jagged dream
That tears all paper truth to shreds
And cuts its line from heart to head."

Andalus nodded gravely when
She spoke these words, to show that he
Agreed, could fully comprehend
And yet, with due humility
Would not pretend to grasp the scope
Of what she knew. He only hoped
She saw in him enough respect
For her travails, could not detect

The baser elements within
That clotted nobler aims, obscured
His own desire for knowledge, pure
Within his art, (should he begin
To trust himself and less his bouts
With melancholy and self-doubt).

"If you would please allow me to
Explain myself and why I've come
I hope you'll sense that there's a true
Respect for what you do, not some
Presumption I could sound the deep
Reserves of wisdom that you keep
Upon your shelves, for those are why
If truth be told, I thought I'd try
To see if there was any way
That we could talk. For as the son
Of one who'd kept such books and run
From Inquisition's reach, I'd pray
You take me for a secret friend
Come here for what perhaps you'd lend."

"My books? The very source of all
The work I practice and believe?"
She laughed. Not even if he crawled
From Trebizond, sent to retrieve
The works once thought as precious, lost
When swords and scimitars had crossed
(Compelling those enlightened few
Who kept these ancient texts and knew
That exile was the only hope
To save these volumes from the flames)
Would she have trusted him. The same
Detachment of the misanthrope
His master had he saw in her,
Yet he knew not to be deterred.

Yes, the books you can't live without. My father's Pushkin, Gogol, and Herzen (his favourite) were all I took with me to Rome, upon my mother's urging. "Your father and I don't need those in this house anymore, and in any case when would your father read them again?" I read them again and again over the years, as if they concealed, in the language of my parents, secrets they could never tell.

And I suppose those books did. They are all that remain on my one bookshelf. I've given every other book away, one to each person who has come to visit.

He reached within a slit he'd made
Inside his belt, produced a note,
And with a solemn nod he laid
It by the scribblings that she wrote
On pages by her pots and vials
Meant to record the careful trial-
And-error struggles of her days
Where transmutations in each phase
Required an eye so sharp, precise.
The painter's skill to mix and grind
His colours was in truth aligned
Completely with this exercise.
That much Andalus knew, for more
This note would have to answer for.

"This note is from my father who
Has knowledge of the secret code
Confirming all I've said as true,
In mirror-text, his Latin flowed
As if an oracle possessed
Him, but I'll let these words attest
To what could be his legacy
Should baseless claims of heresy
Evaporate within these years.
My humble work of shade and light

Could possibly transcend the trite
And tried approaches of my peers.
And with the paintings I complete
I serve his art, past self-defeat."

She slowly took the note in hand
And brought it to her looking glass.
Her lips moved; she could understand
Each Latin word her finger passed
And with a softened look, she seemed
To take them in with new esteem.
The actor curtly nodded, quick
To puff himself. No crone could prick
His self-anointed status of
The poet too in love with truth
To sing to power instead of youth,
Who chose the darker path above
The market streets of easy trade
(The one role he had ably played).

"Your father's words reveal a mind
Who's studied well this sacred code.
That he knew well enough to find
Me here suggests the thoughts that flowed
Upon this page are his alone,
Recounting phases of the stone
Observed and truly understood.
And yet ... there's no way that I could
Just let you take out of my hands
These texts, for there is not a day
That they don't guide me in my way
Of working. He would understand.
What I propose is that you come
To work here when each day is done."

"In increments of evening hours,
Among the staggered, glum parade

Of men who come here, stripped of powers.
To understand how love is made,
I'll let you learn while at my side
To watch each stage, as time provides
Within the phases of the moon
As true a form as one that's hewn
From waves that pound upon a shore.
The transmutations of the stone
Require the skills that one must hone.
Yet once revealed, it's like a door
Is finally opened, you walk through
To golden light, and see anew."

One night Farrell and I had taken Harry to see how the paintings were coming along. Farrell hoped that Tomassoni could warm to Harry's charms and, instead of abandoning the young painter once he had completed his commissions, we could both feel better knowing Tomassoni was on his way to a profitable, if illicit, career working with Harry. The visit was awkward. Ranuccio bristled at Harry's "stravaganza," referred to him in our company as "your friend the pimp" and sullenly worked away in silence, responding to Harry's questions in monosyllables. We wisely took our leave after a quarter of an hour.

Not far from Termini Station, near the garage where Tomassoni did his work, was the Via Salaria, where the "women of the evening", in Farrell's words, congregated. Harry, not a man to let one failed opportunity ruin an evening, insisted we take a seat on the patio of Scherzo, a dingy tavern where we could watch the action. "I wish your young friend Ranuccio was with us now. He thinks he's become a prostitute? He would never have the guts ..." There we sat for the next two hours, drinking "Mexicanos," a bittersweet tequila and amaro cocktail that was apparently the house special, while we watched the action. There was a rickety velodrome nearby where we knew a lot of gambling went on, and once the races were over for the night I watched a stream of clients for the ladies appear, a glum parade of the lucky ones who had made a bit of money. It was fascinating for a while, until the prurience of this whole adventure set in. One couldn't drink too many Mexicanos without feeling a little nauseous.

But Harry was transfixed. He was watching it all like a naturalist on the veldt, waiting for the hyenas and the jackals to surround a herd of beautiful but doomed creatures. "You see all this, my friends? You can talk of politics and painting all night. Here's how it all works."

Nothing I have seen or lived through in the decades since has given me any reason to disagree. It is all a question of vantage point, perhaps, and where you choose to look.

The actor nudged Andalus and
Gave him the look that gamblers know
To mean, "You've got the winning hand,
So play it, then collect and go."
Andalus smiled, and duly trilled
His gratitude, and then, instilled
With all the confidence he'd need,
Said his goodbye and took the lead
To squire his Virgil through the streets,
Concealing his delight until
They could return to drink their fill
And maybe risk an indiscreet
Confession he could not withhold,
For he had never been so bold.

Once they had drunk to his success
And newfound friendship, both surprised
By their connection, as if blessed
With talents for dark enterprise,
Andalus drew him close and said
With an affected tone of dread,
"I have to tell you, now that I
Have got this done. That note's a lie.
My father and I haven't been
On speaking terms for years. I'm just

My master's errand boy, who must
Be careful never to be seen
Involved with this. He wrote that code
And sent me off, with faith bestowed."

The actor could but force a smile
And ruefully admire his friend's
Dissembler's talents, grace, and style,
The noble means, the dubious ends.
"You make me realize that I
In all my years have not asked why
My meagre skills could not be put
To better use, like what's afoot
Within your studio. But be
As cautious as you can, and trust
Yourself. It's rare that for the just
The muses smile. No alchemy
Can alter such a stubborn fact."
Andalus simply nodded back.

9
Nigredo
PART IV

'Enchantment's gaudy enterprise:' Niccolo purchases the
winding sheet, an alleged relic from the Holy Lands, that Leonardo
will use to create the shroud.

Niccolo, after several days
From when Andalus found this crone
Was, eager for his master's praise,
Off on an errand of his own.
Yet knowledge, even of the kind
The fledgling artist hoped to find
Was not the object of his quest.
Sent off to Rome for what was blessed
(Despite all dubious provenance
From lands the Ottomans now claimed)
As relics worthy of their fame,
He'd pay up for such evidence
The son of God had walked the earth
And lived as one of humble birth.

A thriving business was in place
For those who made the pilgrimage
To Rome, and who would take on face
All manner of His "real" image

Along with those of lesser saints.
The church might sanction who could paint
Or sculpt the work that kept in thrall
The flock, yet it could not lure all
The poor benighted souls within
The city of these ancient shades
Without some clever underplayed
Inducement through the harmless sin
Of trade in holy merchandise:
Enchantment's gaudy enterprise.

For wasn't this, in point of fact
What Innocent, for all his airs
And lordly ways had really asked
Lorenzo to procure? The wares
On offer for the pilgrims here
Among the desperate squalor near
The crumbling Capitol's remains,
For all their artlessness, attained
That aura of the real, if just
As proof that even travesty
Possessed an earthy majesty
Lorenzo had insisted must
(Perhaps to spite the Pope's designs)
Be what, at root, this work defined.

To start from such a tawdry source
To fashion Innocent's request
Would for Medici's eyes of course
Put genius to a greater test.
Niccolo sensed, as this was planned
Despite Lorenzo's curt command
A glint of mischief in his eye
For what he had in mind to try:
A challenge for his favoured one
Who'd left his court but not his heart

And had no rival in the arts
Yet still had not in truth begun
To do his talents justice or
Let his imagination soar.

And so Niccolo found himself
With nothing but an old address
Of one who once had served a Guelph
Estate, but through his own excess
With gambling and wine had lost
His tutor's robes, headlong was tossed
Into this world where, like the glass
He sold as "pilgrim mirrors" cast
Refracted rays of sunlit hours
And better ages, nobler ways
And trapped his memories of days
When, like the saints, his earthly powers
Held promise of his soul's ascent
Beyond his master's government.

This man had Gallicized his name
Attributing it to the time
He spent in Paris, (so he claimed)
Where noble courts had deemed it rhyme
With that stark English word *police*.
Fabrizio had become Fabrice,
And yet, for all his artfulness
Averting states of bleak duress
He'd earned a notoriety
For tales he'd tell to hock his wares
And poetry he'd spout to snare
Both high and low society.
So meagre scraps of cloth and bone
Became as gold from painted stone.

These little pilgrim mirrors actually existed. Those who made pilgrimages to holy sites believed if you held up one of these mirrors to a relic, you could trap some of its essence, and it would take on a kind of totemic power as a keepsake, long after you had returned to your somewhat less holy existence. This conception of what the image can convey was the basis for the trade in relics, the one that Innocent in Ocular *tries to leverage to greater purpose.*

Of course there still are pilgrims with their mirrors. Just last summer I attempted, once again, to overcome my hatred of airplanes and airports and flew from Shannon to Milan. Once there I set out for Santa Maria della Grazie on this July morning where you could already feel in the first light of dawn how heavy and oppressive the heat was going to be, and I found myself hoping for just a few stray clouds to form in the sky and block the sun. I made my way through the throng of Korean, Russian, Japanese and American tourists jostling for just one moment of a clear glimpse. I looked up and all I could see were arms raised with their little cameras – these new pilgrim mirrors – as they clicked away. It was a gesture like a kind of prayer, I suppose, full of hope and promise that something transcendent would be saved from this moment, and that it would last and provide them with some validation they were in the presence of a divine power.

In my first trips through the Vatican Collection with Ranuccio Tomassoni, he too carried that expensive German camera he had, as if it would capture something of the genius of his heroes: Caravaggio, Titian, Michelangelo. He did not really trust me that he had special privileges to snap away. He would pull the camera out of his small leather satchel before every painting as if he was taking out an instrument that would steal the souls within each work. Perhaps his intuitions were correct after all.

Niccolo found the cavernous
And cluttered room he called his shop
Along a route notorious
For where the gullible would drop
Each smattering of coins they'd saved,

Their weariness and hunger staved
Off by their innocent belief
That just a glimpse, however brief,
Could be preserved within each glass
They carried to a holy site,
Transmuting presence to a rite
With just the mirror's cursory pass,
The image they beheld retained
Forever, like a spirit chained.

He ran his ink-stained fingers through
The ones that hung from silken threads
Along a curtain rod. A few
Felt heavy as stones from the lead
Fabrice had painted on one side.
They spun and glimmered as he eyed
The squares of silvered light they made
Across the wall before they'd fade
Like stars that glowed in morning skies
He still so vividly could see
From early childhood days when he
Was made to slowly memorize
The constellations one by one
Before the first rays of the sun.

Fabrice, who'd fall asleep each day
In afternoon's pale empty hour
Awoke and squinted through the play
Of light and masked his urge to glower
Upon this whelp who looked as if
He'd scrounged a pittance for a gift
He promised his beloved when
He left for Rome and here, since then
He'd walked the streets, his innocence
Apparent as his poverty,
Unsettled by the liberty

That briefly made him feel a prince
Among the desperate throng that packed
The square, the thieves that he'd attract.

I based Fabrice on Fabrizio Longhi, an acolyte of Harry Maes who loved all things French, and who had moved quickly, after Harry's death, to insinuate himself as a man of influence with Antony Farrell. Anything Harry Maes could do for Farrell, Longhi had said that he could provide.

Longhi claimed he had once been a ballet dancer of some talent, spotted by Balanchine when he performed with Ignazio Filippo's troupe in Paris. He was also rumoured to have had some kind of relationship with Cocteau during his time in Paris. He ended up as a gallery assistant for Harry in Milan, where he gained forty pounds and grew his ginger hair to a ridiculous length. He was a man who combined the most transparent ambitiousness with absolute fecklessness.

Harry was a quick judge of character. He had to be; his times did not allow him the luxury of choosing the wrong people to work with, given there were at least two countries where there was a warrant for his arrest. (Turkey was one of them, and if they had a warrant for Harry's arrest, it is quite possible they had one for my father and everyone from Vidler's auction house.) Fabrizio had to be useful in at least some way or else Harry would have discarded him quickly.

It was less about him than about those he knew. Longhi had an uncle who was very close to Il Duce himself, and he made sure Harry could travel in and out of Italy freely, and that his precious cargo was never subject to the rigorous scrutiny the Blackshirts gave all foreigners, out of a deeply held belief they were looting Rome's antiquities every chance they got.

In exchange for this, Fabrizio could plan out his scenes each morning as he performed the role of Francophile connoisseur. He honed his act for the older ladies who requested he help them out with their estates and humoured them in their neuroses. He was a kind of court eunuch but he was intensely loyal to Harry Maes and his clientele.

What ultimately explains Longhi's presence in Harry's life was something a lot simpler than you can imagine: they were both heroin addicts. Harry knew he was being watched all the time. He was not going to stack the deck against himself by letting his habit dictate the kinds of neighbourhoods he'd frequent and the business arrangements he'd come to in his off hours. What Longhi truly knew about art was questionable. This was my point to Antony, who gave Longhi more time than he deserved. But he was useful despite himself, ensuring that Harry had a steady supply of what he needed to function.

Not long after Harry's death Fabrizio had made his play for working with Antony Farrell, but it failed predictably – you couldn't lie about yourself; Farrell could see it in your eyes. Fabrizio was well on his way to becoming a footnote in this whole story. He probably never knew how close he came to being targeted for murder himself because of his indiscretion about the MI6-Vatican plot. He told more than a few people in Milan that he had been asked to secretly help the Curia in its plans to sell off fakes of the Vatican collection to this new German clientele. Perhaps he was lucky that no one took him seriously.

I was in Paris for the wedding of Connie Vidler's daughter to Didier Binet in '87, when I read an obit in Le Monde *for a Fabrizio Longhi of Paris. He was described as the editor of* Editions Hurtebise, *a publishing house that was in existence until 1975. It was an imprint with a rather small list of authors, though Philippe Sollers was quoted as calling Fabrizio Longhi a "legendary figure" among a milieu that was vanishing in Paris, a man who still had an ear "for the particular music of the French we spoke before television and American movies," and who cultivated writers who could still capture it on the page.*

So perhaps he was more of a survivor than I imagined, and more of a legitimate aesthete as well. This Fabrizio Longhi could have been a completely different man, but I would like to believe that he had finally found some talent he could claim for himself.

"Can I be of some service? You
Appear to have some interest in
A glass … or have you come to view
The relics that I keep within
That private room?" With just a nod
He gestured past the garish, flawed

Approximation of a door
Filched from a Lycian tomb, from shores
The Turks defended that was brought
By merchant seamen for the Pope
As proof of conquest, in the hope
They would remain first in his thoughts
Should there be talk of some campaign.
(There wasn't – they'd returned in vain.)

The door was based on an artifact smuggled out of Kas, Turkey, which became one of Harry Maes's most audacious forgeries.

One of Goebbels's flacks, Helmuth Wittig, had become a collector and client of Harry's. He had recently married into the Krups family fortune and was eager to purchase some taste. He was a dull, plump fellow with a spaniel's eyes and the full lips of a teenage girl. He had the melancholy air of a man permanently aggrieved. I don't believe he ever bought a piece of art that was actually for him. It all seemed to be motivated by some desire to please his father-in-law, whom he affectionately called "das Ungeheuer" (the ogre).

Wittig was in Paris in the first two years of the Occupation, and he became enamoured with Rodin's Gates of Hell. *Harry had found him a couple of small sculptures attributed to Rodin's studio – which were most likely fake – and Wittig was so pleased he recommended Harry to a number of clients of higher rank and wealth. For Harry, Wittig was an intermediary to a whole new market. I had presumed it would have been a relationship so valuable he would have never done anything to jeopardize it. But that wasn't Harry. The contempt he held for Wittig was palpable when he spoke of him. He said he would do anything to cheat him. The beauty of it lay in the fact that Wittig seemed constitutionally incapable of revenge.*

So one afternoon, when we were in the Vidler warehouse out near Ostia, he had his moment of inspiration. He had spied two of the doors my father managed to purchase from his tour of the Lycian tombs along the Turkish coast and he let out a loud "Hah!"

Fabrizio tittered.

I watched Harry as he quickly marched over to examine the doors.
I could hear that little gasp he let out when he found something that
amused or delighted him. Harry was not a big man, and he usually
looked as sleek as a greyhound in his bespoke suits and pomaded hair,
so I was shocked by the way he manhandled those old doors. They had
to weigh at least two hundred pounds each but he turned them this
way and that, examining the edges, the panels, the ornate, hand-carved
designs engraved on the cedar. He nudged and heaved them along a
vacant space of wall until he could look at them under a solitary light
bulb. There he studied them in silence for about five minutes. I watched
him smoke down a cigarette in what seemed just a couple of drags. Then
from behind I could see the tension dissipate across his bony shoulder
blades, his hips ease into this cocksure pose as he turned and said "They're
perfect! I must have them for Wittig!"

He asked me to ship them to a studio out in Allerona, this village near
Orvieto where I knew he had one of his better artists who specialized in
Renaissance work like Tomassoni. He had a model in mind – Ghiberti's
Gates of Paradise *– and a book of photographs from Rodin's studio that*
he took with him as he packed up his things in his Bugatti and vanished
out into the countryside. Harry never told you when he would be back,
never told you where he would be from one week to the next. He would
breeze through his gallery to get what he needed and make sure Longhi
was minding the books and then he would be off again, telling no one
his itinerary.

About three months later, as Antony and I were having a drink with
Harry in one of those piazzas in Trastevere that used to be so beautiful
and serene, he pulled out a stack of photographs of those doors. They
were unrecognizable, transformed into the creaking figments of a
Renaissance imagination – or at least Rodin's version of a Renaissance
imagination. Harry had just shipped them to Paris, telling Wittig they
were relics from Ghiberti's studio that had just been uncovered in a
barn near Florence. This was better than another Rodin; it was work
that inspired the great sculptor after all. Wittig paid a fortune for them.

"That door looks like a gate from hell,
Whatever lies behind it must
Be what you'd only come to sell
To those who'd earned your deepest trust."
Niccolo raised his hand to shield
His eyes – a gesture that concealed
His own self-consciousness about
This role he now was playing out;
Yet nothing seemed to faze Fabrice.
He figured him an easy read,
One gullible enough to bleed
For more than he could usually fleece
From men of stature who had learned
A gift for love was not love earned.

"Allow me to invite you in
For I can tell you've got an eye
And know the special power within
Each sacred relic found and why
Who buys each piece can matter more
'Than all the golden coins that pour
Into my hand, when I have sold
A piece that is at least as old
As all this city's built upon.
The one to whom I sell this work
Must be the kind that wouldn't shirk
His duty to an age beyond
His own, and so in faith preserves
It like the wealth that he deserves."

He brought him to an oaken chest
Then took the keys from 'round his neck
And crossed himself along his breast
While mumbling Latin to protect
Their souls as they beheld these few
Choice relics that Niccolo knew

Would offer him such little scope
To choose, for he would have to hope
Lorenzo would be pleased by what
Would form the basis of the piece
That would provide him the release
From any purchase in the plot
Of Innocent's corrupt design –
The blackened blood poured out as wine.

And there behold, each relic 'cased
In glass and nestled on a bed
Of scarlet silk and squarely placed
So nobody could be misled
Into believing more was there
Than these: a tooth, a lock of hair,
A torn scrap from a winding sheet
That bore the imprint of the feet
Supposedly of Saint Matthew.
In fact they all had different names
Of tombs inscribed as where they came
From, so at least one could be true,
Niccolo graciously surmised,
While feigning something like surprise.

With those he brought out from the chest
Fabrice, with calculating eye
Was taking note how each impressed
This boy, which one he'd want to buy.
And as he brought the fabric from
The winding sheet out, there was some
Of that familiar focus he
Had seen so many times to be
The telltale sign of imminent
Decision, so he just sat back,
Allowed Niccolo to react
As he expected, flame from flint,

Endearing almost, as the words
Began to form, sweet music heard.

"This scrap of winding sheet you've got
From Matthew's tomb I'd like to own.
But as you've guessed, it's true I'm not
Much more than just a servant known
For my ambition, I believe,
Who still has so much to achieve,
I'm told, before I could expect
To prove, to any great effect
My counsel is of value to
The Curia, yet if they saw
In me a kind of tragic flaw
That I cannot resist a few
Choice tokens of the sacred word
Made flesh, my path will be assured.

"What I'm suggesting is a start
To a relationship that could
Be one that would play no small part
In working towards our mutual good.
I may be one of meagre means
At present, but I haven't seen
A rival for the favour of
The men who'll vault me far above
My humble station soon enough.
And if you'd grant a cut in price
For this initial piece, a nice
Arrangement could – for all this stuff –
Be made, that would ensure for years
To come, an old age without tears."

Fabrice could not suppress a smirk;
A laugh escaped his mouth as he
Surveyed his slipshod handiwork,

His one claim to posterity.
He couldn't help admire the gall
Of this upstart who, but for all
His confidence, could surely pass
For yet another dull outcast
Who'd saved his wages for a gift
His poor beloved future wife
Would for the rest of her sad life
Mark as the moment when the swift,
Unerring dart from Cupid's quill
Had struck, just as bad poets trill.

This boy had something more than pluck,
A fearlessness so rare it seemed
He'd surely make his own good luck
Regardless of his rivals' schemes
To bring him down, a kind of prince
Of his own making ... so, convinced
This boy was surely worth the cut
In profit now, he firmly shut
The case that held the winding sheet
And looked him squarely in the eye.
"I trust you, though I'm not sure why
I sense no practice of deceit
Within your charms. I'll take the chance.
You've called the tune. Pay for the dance."

Niccolo smiled and nodded as
He fumbled for his coins within
The pocket where he kept the last
Few left Lorenzo gave to him.
"You know you won't regret this
Yet I'm sure some written oath is,
Though unasked for, still in accord
With how you live – not by the sword.
So let me write this simple note

That you can hold me to until
When, either in old age or killed
In some adventure I'll devote
Myself to in the years ahead,
That I'll live up to what I've said."

This note within a box he kept
High on a bookshelf, then he plucked
The crisp notes that Niccolo left
Upon the trunk while counting to
Himself, then walked Niccolo through
The Lycian door and shook his hand.
Niccolo couldn't understand
How quickly all the pleasantries
Had been acquitted by his host
Until he vanished like a ghost
With just the jangle of his keys
From 'round his neck, the final sound
That brought a threadbare curtain down.

Albedo

PART I

Leonardo meets with his old patron, Lorenzo de Medici, in Milan.
A conversation follows about the "real" commission for the artist.

A satire, slowly, word by word
Had in Milan begun to take
Its form from what Niccolo heard
From his new master, come to stake
His claim for peace and true accord
On matters that their states had warred
For generations, so they claimed,
(The lists of allies, foes unnamed).
Niccolo watched him while they dined
As guests of Sforza, come to stay
For what was dubbed "the only way
Our interests will remain aligned."
So said Lorenzo, as he stood
Almost convinced, for his own good.

His motives might indeed be just
For summering here, shy, but in tow,
His daughter, who had all the trust
That he could summon (or she know
Again within her troubled life

As Franceschetto's ill-starred wife)
and the son-in-law himself, come
As eyes for Innocent, whose glum
Oppressive thuggishness was clear
To all around him while he tried
To force a smile from those he eyed
As conquests during his time here,
For what else could distract his thoughts
Of veiled betrayals and counterplots?

He thought upon what lurked within
The chambers of Lorenzo's heart,
The prince of all these hypocrites,
And as these trite resentments stoked
The furnace of his bastard's rage
He couldn't see the trails of smoke
From other fires while thus engaged.
The looks from Leonardo's boy
Directed at his wife, whose coy
And winsome smile, with eyes downcast
Provoked a scribbled message passed
Her way, which she at once concealed
Within her underskirt, to read
Once she was off alone and freed
To be herself, the girl she sealed
Off from the world the day she wed,
Her heart a book of love unread.

Yes, I am aware of the questionable imagery when I write of dark skin signifying a treacherous character and inscrutability. Yet there is a historical basis for all of this; Ludovico Sforza's complexion did indeed really earn him the nickname of "il Moro," or the Moor, and those connotations were real. And Leonardo was working for him.

The detail is there for more than simply a pedantic adherence to historical record. It said something about Leonardo's priorities: he went

where the work and the money were most favourable, regardless of his
ties to Lorenzo and Florence. And he would move from one court to
another for the rest of his life, loyal to one guiding faith throughout: his
vision and the artistic gifts he was blessed with. He had a mind that,
perhaps in a perpetual torment, could not be but obsessed with all that
produced shape and form and beauty out of chaos and darkness.

The kind of ego, talent, and ambition Leonardo embodied always
finds the money and the means to create. Circumstance may weigh
heavily on the mediocre and this is why politics unfortunately matters,
but for those who can wager on immortality, circumstances are merely
the constraints that create the required tension and complexity
within the work. This I always wanted to tell the Martin O'Reillys of
the world: politics can never explain away a Leonardo, in the way it
can a Medici, a Machiavelli, or an Andalus.

Or yes, maybe even a Tomassoni.

He also missed Lorenzo's nod
In the direction of the door
To Leonardo as he trod
Upon the stage's petalled floor
Declaring that the nuptials of
The masquers who declared their love –
One named Milana, one Firenze,
Had now been sealed, and peaceful ends
Had sanctified such artful means
To sound the harmonies of state
And *polis*, who had come of late
To see the wiles deemed Byzantine
In cities southward of the Po
As seeds for blackened souls to sow.

Not even such an overt slight
Did Franceschetto comprehend
And as Lorenzo went from sight
All he deduced was that an end

To all of the festivities
Might be at hand, and if he seized
This moment to escape the bonds
Of wife and family to abscond
With wine enough to quench his thirst,
He could set out into the streets
And with a little luck he'd meet
Those who'd indulge him at his worst.
He rose to leave, then walked right through
The courtyard of the rendezvous.

Lorenzo mentioned in a note
Dispatched to Leonardo when
He had arrived they must devote
Some time to speak of art again.
No more than this had to be said
For both knew where such talks had led
When Leonardo graced his court,
The challenges, declared in sport
Were never quite as innocent
Of baser motives that befit
The man who had without remit
To think of less benevolent
Pursuits than chasing down the muse –
These mild requests were not refused.

With just a quick embrace the years
That had elapsed since they had met
Dissolved, though it was gravely clear
To Leonardo, with regret
The lines that creased the corners of
Lorenzo's eyes spoke less of love,
An ageing man's domestic bliss,
Than of transactions once dismissed
As doses of corruption downed
In increments, each brimming spoon,

With no awareness that so soon
The poison turns a body sound
To one the surgeons hang their heads
O'er, leave for those who rob the dead.

Yet this was not the time to call
To mind Lorenzo's choice of words
The years had been as stern to all
His friends in rendering absurd
Ideals pristine, unsullied by
The grit of compromise, the "I"
That once declared he'd not be tamed
For any court, had felt his fame
So alter whom he looked upon
When faced with what the mirror showed,
That he could not presume to know
Who that man was; his eye was gone
And so he'd come to question what
Were called his gifts. A door had shut

Upon the past; yet here he was
Within this courtyard face to face
With his first patron, and because
Some things just could not be erased
By time or the imperatives
He clung to – so declarative
When writing down what he induced –
That now he felt once more reduced
To who he'd been when first they met:
The boy whose eagerness to please
And careless charm dispelled unease
Perhaps too well with strangers, yet
He was the most deceptive to
His better self – the self he knew.

"I knew there must be some veiled plot

For you to claim the time was right
To listen closely, share your thoughts
With Sforza each and every night
For weeks until you ... what, define
How interests will remain aligned?
You know it's hardly credible.
You're lucky that his head is full
With plans for his ascendancy
Among the statesmen who can claim
A true dominion in their name.
It's made my own dependency
Upon his favour, sad to say,
Hard to resist, for Sforza pays."

"And I did not?" Lorenzo laughed.
"Or did I underestimate
Your value, treating like a craft
All that you laboured to create?
If that was once indeed the case
Let me suggest I now have learned
That you have always more than earned
The patronage of lesser men.
Yet now's the time that we again
Should work for mutual benefit.
I know it's as an engineer
That Sforza's kept you busy here
But what if Maddalena sits
For you to paint for me? Would you
Have time to see the portrait through?"

"There's time enough if what you need
Is nothing that I'd have to claim
As little more than an agreed
Upon confection in my name.
If she can come and sit each day
For several hours, there's a way

That something like a portrait might
Be rendered, though why such a trite
Addition to the works you own
Would come to mind when think how long
It's been … of course I'll go along
With what you'd ask. It's you alone
Responsible for where I am.
You saved me, back when I was damned."

"Enough. No need to talk of then.
You never were one for the past,
There's one thing more I'll hope you'll spend
Some time on while this sojourn lasts.
It will require much more than just
This painter's task that I entrust
You with, in fact it must o'erleap
That shaded ground where muses sleep
And vault beyond, into the real:
An image that could be believed
As sacred – this must be achieved.
You know the Roman fools who deal
In relics? Well, I've now become
That greater fool who'll foot the sum."

This refers to an incident that occurred in Florence when Leonardo was apprenticed to a painter named Verocchio. He and a few others were expelled from the studio because of their homosexuality. The adjective "Florentine" was used as slang for those who engaged in this unlawful carnal knowledge. Even Lorenzo distanced himself, with as much credibility as possible, from a milieu he was very much a part of.

I never spoke to Farrell about his abrupt departure from the priesthood, the network of priests and cardinals who had ensured he got an education that honed his talents and then a position in the Vatican. Like Leonardo, an early scandal could have even been a calculated move to ensure he would always be looked after – as long as he remained useful.

Lorenzo's smirk to mask his shame,
The gaze so fixed upon the floor
Said more about the statesman's games
He had to play – that he abhorred –
Than any further wan attempt
At irony, enough contempt
For Innocent's unholy reign
Was clear, he did not have to feign
A subtle rationale for this.
A painter with true grace and style
Would render Maddalena's smile
A parody of wedded bliss,
The "real" work that he needed done
Was for the role penned for his son.

"Far be it for a reprobate
Like me to see in such a task
Some merit, but in truth of late
My work might speak to what you ask.
Some time ago I found that I
Could frankly not remember why
A painter's life with all its tired
Concerns had ever once inspired
Me to devote the countless hours
Obsessing over light and shade
And how the right effects were made
Within each frame. My meagre powers
With line and form have never shown
Much progress – this I've always known.

"And yet I cannot simply stop
To think about the ways one could
Produce a work so real each drop
Of paint can serve some higher good.
I will not bore you with the trials
And botched experiments done while

You've made your legacy your sole
Concern. I'll only say the whole
Obsession's led me to a void:
What's simply called a camera
I've fashioned where ephemera,
The images my work's destroyed
Time and again, can actually be
Suspended in the dark to see."

Lorenzo smiled and tried to look
As if such talk kept him enthralled
While knowing Leonardo took
His act as politesse, a small
But well-remembered nod
To when the only kind of God
That gave them pause to think and speak
Was one translated from the Greek,
From volumes brought from Trebizond.
If all of that was in the past
when both of them held strong and fast,
These books would long survive beyond
their time. Now immortality
Was trumped by stark reality.

"You know – whatever that it takes
For you to make a pilgrim weep
If it's a catacomb of fakes
You have to burn for one to keep,
I'll happily indulge you 'til
You manage something that could still
The beating hearts of plebian
And Pope alike, so deep within
The Curia which, let me say,
Despite my all too lavish words
For how they've managed the absurd
Have done their best to bar the way

For my son to, in time, ascend
The throne before my life will end.

"But please don't think on all of that.
I let my tongue be ruled by all
The pettiness that by fiat
Will soon enough be my downfall."
A nod from Leonardo quelled
These thoughts, he briefly clasped and held
His hand in his and made him feel
That in these darker times a real
Connection to those better days
That both of them had left behind
Existed and that these designs
Might lead them as if through a maze
Back to the past, that meadow burned
To blackened earth, where none returned.

Farrell had written a thesis on the influence of alchemy on painting methods. He was a rich source of information for both Harry and me in determining how to make a forgery undetectable. But I think he had an even greater influence on me in one respect; he helped shape my views on power and art beyond the force and charisma of Harry's personality (I don't think Harry would have ever consciously converted anyone to his survivor's creed). My reading on the Renaissance had ground the lens for me to see how power intersects with the making of a masterpiece, but my walks within the Vatican with Antony were at least as powerful an awakening. Trust a man like him, who had lost his religion but had rediscovered a Machiavellian faith, to find his ideal convert in such a perpetual innocent as me.

One evening after Mass Farrell told me of the plan in advance of the "errand" MI6 had given him. This would be the spring of '42. I had just returned from Aosta where, for the sake of a sale, I had gone on a weekend climb of Gran Paradiso with one of my clients and the partner in his law firm, a pudgy mama's boy who kept me in cognac and cigarettes

*through the worst of it. I called him Sancho Panza. Anyway, I felt like
I had been stretched on a rack and could barely walk; my calves were as
hard as Indian rubber. I was tired, made weary of always being "on,"
pretending to be interested in the banal pursuits of these men with too
much money, with their weaknesses for actresses and cabaret dancers.
What a relief to be out with Antony, talking of all he was witnessing
within the Vatican as Pius deliberated on how far he would go to cooperate
with the Germans.*

*We were heading to the Café Greco when he turned to me and
mumbled, "We should talk about the Curia, Nicholas, have a little chat
if we can get a table near the back. They have a request you're going to
hear about."*

*All my weariness, all the stiffness in my legs and shoulders eased with
the surge of adrenalin coursing through me. I felt dangerous and valuable.
I felt alive again.*

*Once we had sat down beside a couple of schoolgirls with their
governess, it seemed to me we'd be safe to speak of anything we liked
in English, but Farrell wasn't taking any chances. Without taking a
breath he began speaking to me in Latin. It flowed so naturally with
him. All the strained, flutey mid–Atlantic pretensions of his accent that
he adopted to conceal his Irish origins were gone. A darker, guttural tone
emerged.*

*Some individuals within the Curia had serious reservations about
the direction Pius was heading, he said. He anticipated my question,
tapped his fingers on the top of my hand. "Don't ask. Just listen." These
men worried about how fawning Pius had been to the Nazis who had
come calling. They feared what would be lost. They had a sense of how
these barbarians would relish plundering all of enduring value, deciding amongst themselves what would look best on their walls. "But you
know and I know," he said, "from all Harry's told us, you can sell these
amentibi [idiots?] practically anything if you have the documents of its
provenance and a name of a painter they recognize daubed in the corner
of the canvas."*

*"Why come to me? Why not go to Harry? This is perfect for him,"
I said.*

He shook his head, allowed the beginnings of a smile to form at the corners of his mouth. I noticed he was growing a wispy little moustache. Perhaps he thought it would give him a look of more authority. "That's what MI6 will suggest. I just think Harry's too close with the Germans. He can't be trusted."

Long after I had written Ocular *and Farrell had taken Tomassoni's paintings with him to Ireland for this travesty of an exhibition we organized for him, it occurred to me that Farrell might have been MI6 as well, rather than simply doing Quigley's and Delegarde's bidding. Those bastards knew me well enough to realize if they'd sent some other flunky to get me to carry out these orders, I could hardly be trusted to accomplish them on their timelines or with any real discretion.*

What was worse, MI6 would be the ones with the greatest interest in burying a Tomassoni's career – and that was necessary. It was like something taken from the blackest of comedies to presume his "Catholic art" would garner any attention in Dublin. Farrell maintained that anyone who knew anything about art got out of that city as soon as they were able, a view that justified his own exile, of course.

Farrell remained vague about who within the Curia was giving Quigley and Delegarde orders. Was it simply one priest or was there some cabal at work? All I could be sure of was that money to pay for the forged work would not be a problem. Such an embezzlement of funds would have required great authority if it remained undetected – or perhaps the money simply came from a different source, one much closer to me than I would have speculated upon at the time.

Farrell and I set out one afternoon within the Vatican to examine some of the works for which we needed forgeries made. There would be ten works initially commissioned for forgery. Those chosen would reflect a diversity of styles and genres rather than some selection of the greatest work the Vatican possessed. Once completed, Delegarde would review and decide how many more they would fund, how bold they could be about passing off something, say, Tomassoni had done as a Caravaggio. They hoped at least one hundred paintings could be "saved." But what if those first ten were too poorly done to pass as the originals? We realized it was a gamble; we would pay the commissions regardless of the outcome. "*If you can just find the talent to accomplish this, all will be well,*" Antony said. "*I trust you, and they will, too, in time.*"

I said I could easily find two or three painters who could get this done. In fact I really only knew of Tomassoni and of van Meegeren, working out of his hideaway in Roquebrune-Cap-Martin, and I had no clue how I was going to contact him without dealing with Harry. But I wasn't going to admit that to anyone. Like everything else in my improvised life, I would figure it out myself.

With Tomassoni it was easy enough; he loved boxing. It was the theatricality of a match, I believe – the drama, the suffering, the blood. It is a perfect Catholic sport, isn't it? Bullfighting is too pagan. I took him to an old warehouse on the outskirts of Rome where two Calabrian construction workers were tearing into each other for the gate money. The audience was sharply divided between those who must have known these men and those who looked as if they had just come from the opera and who seemed enchanted by the brutality. Or no – maybe that's not quite accurate – they felt as if they were witnessing something sacred from a primitive culture. I told Tomassoni they would have made a better subject for a painter than the boxers, but he just gave me a smile that could not conceal his condescension.

It was a simple proposition. He and I would meet and examine the suggested paintings in the Vatican collection. I suggested I would bring along a camera so he would have something to work from if he deemed them "paintable." But no, that wouldn't be necessary; he had his own, a Zeiss Ikon some German had left in his uncle's tavern and had never come back to retrieve. For all his talk of how conflicted he was about prostituting his art, he treated the money on offer as incidental. What he really wanted, what he believed I or Farrell could offer him (simply because we were foreigners, presumably wealthy and friends of Harry Maes), was a gallery show of his original work. Ranuccio's ambition and idealism, his belief in his own genius, was so pure and innocent, despite how tough and circumspect he wanted to appear.

It was some years ago, after I had been living in Ireland a few years and started to understand a little of the history, that I realized there was something very Irish in this plan (though Farrell would have been *scornful of me saying so; he seemed to despise his own country). It had happened before after all. During the Dark Ages as Rome was sacked and pillaged, the monks had saved all that could provide the foundations for civilization once again, out here in the farthest reaches of the empire. I just think it far more likely for the Curia to have been thinking in centuries rather than in dark decades ahead – whether MI6 was involved or not.*

And yet, all higher purposes aside, the fact remains that we probably destroyed a man's life and his belief in his own talent. Of course the "exhibition" of his work was a farce, but Tomassoni, who was just barely literate, did not have the learning or the inner resources to persevere in the face of what would no doubt have been years of critical and commercial indifference to his work.

In this postcard I wish Michael Tomassoni had told me what his father's paintings were like. I suspect there were hardly any works Michael inherited, though, perhaps a few landscapes or portraits that showed some talent and more than rudimentary technique. Likely there was really only a story told to this Michael Tomassoni, probably not long before his father died – one that an old Calabrian man couldn't make up – and a few old documents, like this note from an exhibition he claims to have read.

Indeed, why would Ranuccio save much of anything over the years? After the work he accomplished for the Curia, he had nothing left to prove to anyone. He probably always knew that, despite the hopes he once had for his talent.

Albedo

PART II

*Maddalena's first visit to Leonardo's studio, her
meeting Andalus and the beginnings of what will be conceived
of love and art.*

Imagine, in a studio
That looks as barren as the hope
That any one of faith well knows
They'd ever find from Church or Pope
Within this long-corrupt domain,
Imagine one object remains:
A kind of cube that could have served
To cage a man if he deserved
A vanquished tyrant's bitter end,
Four walls as black as starless night
Save for a pinhole where the light
Can enter, focussed by a lens
To form a perfect image of
The object of a painter's love.

It's here where Andalus has toiled
For Leonardo with the aid
Of pigment mixtures ground and boiled
From what Gethsemane has said

And taught him from the books she's kept.
For weeks now Andalus has crept
Back up the stairs within that home
Of quick transactions fit for Rome's
Illustrious sons – like our Cybo
Who, truth be told, has yet to meet
Gethsemane but knows the sweet
Enchantments that remain on show
Well past the hours of Sforza's court,
From ladies sworn not to report

About the guests or what occurred
While they were there, a sacred trust,
If ever one could use that word
With meaning, it obtained for lust
And also kept within those walls
The province of that greater fall
Of souls into the waiting arms
Of pagan practices and charms
The whores had claimed for Magdalene,
The sole apostle who in name
And rites of faith that they could frame
As their protectress, washed of sin,
An icon of their own for prayer
Who kept their souls within her care.

It had become, by way of this
Subversion by necessity
A church so true and blasphemous
It claimed a greater chastity,
Though little of its gospel had
Affected Andalus, just glad
His father's wayward wandering
Meant more than simply squandering
His talents and his better years
Believing that his bookish trade

In time would grow and be parlayed
Into some seat as royal seer
(As tragic and absurd as all
That was, he had not far to fall).

And now, although Andalus longed
To hone his skills and learn from one
Incapable of any wrong
Decision once he had begun
To paint, he knew in time his chance
Would come, to trust that circumstance
Was not the adversary he
Had always feared; he could be free
To take of what he learned here and
With wisdom's gentle irony
Transcend a doomed epigone's
Untimely fate, once he had planned
The moment when he'd stake his claim
And sell a work in his own name.

Content to wait, he felt assured
As Leonardo came to him
To have, he said, "a little word
About the progress of these dim
But palpably defined attempts
To show that, far from the contempt
I've normally reserved for such
Occult beliefs, there is still much
That can be gleaned from these old texts
For what is best to trap the line
And form of images defined
By what a well-placed glass reflects,"
(So read the note he found on this
New series of wrought images).

When finally his master came

To lure him from this little box
He knew, just by the way his name
Was called, this was one of their talks
Preceding a commission that
Would flatter some old kleptocrat
And keep the florins coming in.
The wages from the patron's sins
Was alchemy reversed, for gold
Was not their transmutation's end;
It just allowed them to extend
Themselves with greater means, be "bold
And fearless in their inquiry,"
Was Leonardo's flip decree.

Yet as Andalus had come out
From studying a plate he'd laid
Within this camera, any doubt
That something more than money made
Would come from this diversion were
Expelled. How could he not infer
'This, seeing who accompanied
His master? She, whose look of need
Was something more than just desire?
All talk of what was in the note
Would wait here if he could devote
The full attention she required.
Perhaps his master would allow
Him finally to paint her now.

*If either Farrell or Olivia, my two readers at the time, had asked me
what I had meant by this "something more," I like to think I would
have been honest enough to say I really didn't know. I could have speculated and suggested it was a force that transformed all feelings of sexual
attraction into something more profound. True to some neo-Platonic
ideal of the period of this fiction, maybe I would have suggested that*

Maddalena believed that there was the other half of each soul out there, waiting, like a lock for its key, to be found.

Olivia believed, true to her vocation, that of all the advancements of the so-called Renaissance, the depiction – rather than the invention – of romantic love was of the highest order. When I had finally finished a draft of Ocular, *she wrote me, "I wonder how Maddalena would have written this work. You were right to suggest this is the story told from the perspective of a young Machiavellian. True to your title, from* Othello, *this could be Iago's work, with love 'a lust of the blood and a permission of the will.'"*

Years later, even after her years with Martin O'Reilly and all the struggles she had continuing as a working actor after she was no longer thought desirable, she remained a firm believer in romantic love. She had inherited my father's aristocratic hauteur, despite how hostile she was to his politics. The world was not quite good enough for her idealism. My realism, in contrast, would always mark me as her brother with a callow heart, one who could only love art, not life.

"Andalus, let me introduce
You to the daughter of my friend
Who, as I'm sure you can deduce
Has asked of you and me to spend
Some time to do her justice in
A portrait we must soon begin."
What could he do but smile with her,
Extend this bit of theatre
As she pretended not to know
That he had looked at her with eyes
Which saw her as the greatest prize
That he could claim if he could show
The true intentions of his heart,
As strong and honest as his art?

He bowed and kissed her outstretched hand
While she, with just the gentlest nod

Looked down upon her wedding band.
Perhaps if it was just as flawed
As all that sent her altar-bound
She'd see enough auspicious grounds
For what occurred the moment she
Caught sight of him on bended knee
At Sforza's court, presented to
The guests invited for the masque
Then sent away before she'd asked
If he was Leonardo's new
Diversion, for he'd had his share
Who learned their art within his care.

Yet now that she could feel his gaze
Upon her an unquiet sense
Of what might happen in the days
Ahead left her with no defence.
If she could stay composed, at least
For Leonardo doubts would cease
About her fitness to take on
Her father's legacy and throne
Perhaps, if not in name then deed,
While far from home her brother could
Unite the church for common good.
All this was possible when needs
And appetites forged from desire
Just cooled to steel, clear of this fire.

Maddalena's brother was of course Giovanni, first a Cardinal at thirteen and then Pope Leo X. "Happy families are all alike," the saying goes …

The fact that she now looked away
From Andalus felt like a test
She'd passed, whatever else the day

Presented; nothing else could best
Her and she brightened at this thought,
Relieved that Leonardo brought
Her to her greater sense of self,
The solemn duty to the wealth
Of history her family name
Was freighted with, a burden more
Than lovelessness she calmly bore
While promising herself that shame
To such a legacy pristine
Would not be hers (unless unseen).

"Your father, Maddalena, should
Rest well assured that Andalus
Is more than passably a good
Apprentice. He will dazzle us
In years to come with what his art
Will lead him to achieve. The start
Of what will be a great career
Begins with you, just sitting here
Within our working hours, for though
Your portrait's broad conception will
Be in my hands, my hours are filled
With this within my studio ..."
He gestured to the box to make
It clear it wasn't for his sake.

"So please don't think there's anything
Amiss if I am otherwise
Engaged. The efforts that we'll bring
To this will please your father's eyes
We shall hope, though I'm aware
You're sure to feel as if stripped bare
Before the eyes that hold the brush.
But know that here, within the hush
That will descend within these walls

While we are working, that your trust
In how your portrait's rendered must
Remain inviolate. Not one small
Discomfort you might come to feel
Is yours to bear – or worse, conceal."

Andalus meekly watched this act –
His master's unctuous tone, the bow –
And felt unsure how to react
If called upon, with knitted brow
To nod and mumble his support
While hoping she would not report
To anyone the note he passed
To her when she had seen him last.
For how was he to know that she,
Beyond a mere flirtatious glance,
Would be his partner in this dance
Of innocence, propriety?
The choice was hers to call the steps:
Their roles assigned, their secret kept.

She smiled, but cryptically, and took
Her time to frame within her mind
The quality of light, the look
Of stark industriousness, the lines
Upon the scraps of parchment so
Precise and straight, the way the glow
Of mercury within a glass
Was like a silver tinged with brass
As sunlight washed it, in its place
Upon a window ledge. All seemed
So strangely right, as if she'd dreamed
This very scene, had known the face
Of him who'd be her lover long
Before, the tremor felt so strong.

She breathed in deeply, closed her eyes
As if incapable of thoughts
That might be willfully unwise,
The whims that launched a thousand plots
Of comedies that charmed the court
And made of love a woman's sport
And kept her mildly entertained
Despite herself – for what explained
This sudden urge to run from here?
A chance like this might never come
Again, why would she choose to numb
Herself from what transcended fear?
If this required her to deceive
Her husband, well, no cause to grieve.

And so, when finally she spoke,
She couldn't help but stand just like
Her father, far too bold to cloak
His firm resolve, that same tone spiked
With ironies so sharply honed,
Each word cut close as jeweler's stones,
She spoke of how surprised she'd been
When asked to sit; she'd never seen
Herself as one whose looks compelled
A man to rhapsodize and slip
Those lovestruck thoughts that passed his lips
Into a note, much less beheld
Such proof of his desire, and yet
"What Venus asks of us she gets …"

*But sometimes she doesn't ask. Further to Olivia's comment about the
romantic conception of love in this work: at the time this was written, I
at least believed I could imagine what it was like to be lovestruck. All I
have ever really felt is something like a general contentment about being
someone's companion. Until I didn't anymore, after the third try at it.*

Lust was another thing entirely, and thankfully far more transitory and less emotionally taxing.

Perhaps if I was more attractive, more opportunities would have been available to me. By my forties all the gin and heavy lunches had made me stout. No matter how well cut my suits were, when I looked in the mirror I saw a squat, bespectacled old paper pusher. If I took my bifocals off, too many people said I looked like Charles Laughton. Venus had other appointments to attend to than to call on me. It was not that I lacked courage in seeking out more from all of that; I just lacked belief that it existed.

"Though I would be the last to know,
To see myself within this light
Is not the pose my mirror shows.
To just be good and do what's right
As childish as that surely sounds
Has always been the firmest ground
When left alone I've walked upon
And where I've felt that I belonged.
This terra incognita that
You artists bravely colonize
Is country, you must realize
Where many fear they will combat
Some wilder self from deep within,
The one who dwells outside of sin."

The man whom she was speaking to,
Regardless of the way her gaze
Held firm ... well, Leonardo knew
The thoughts that would infuse her days
Within this studio, and yet
What harm was there if he just let
This girl's infatuation run
Its course? He'd already begun
To paint this portrait in his head

And knew Andalus could complete
It well enough, so he could treat
The greater task beheld with dread
With all the focus it required,
Much more at hand than her desire.

He let her babble on until
She'd found a way to tie her thoughts
Into a bow, aware she still
Was acting as if she forgot
The real addressee stood before
Her, yet that hardly mattered for
The sake of obligation met.
He'd shown her 'round, now they could get
Back to the work at hand within
The camera once she was gone.
Each minute now felt twice as long
As when, escorted, she came in.
He gently clasped her hand to bring
Her back to Sforza's guard, and freed

To do whatever women of
Her age and privilege did alone:
Write letters to their secret loves
Or broken-hearted, pine and moan
For love long unrequited that
Consumed their waking hours, begat
The tiresome songs played for the court
He barely could compose for sport
Yet knew were central to his charm
Among these patrons he required
For means to work on what inspired
Him, so in sum what was the harm?
With self-congratulation he
Knew what he was required to be.

Less self-assured of his designs
Was Andalus now that she'd left.
His confidence felt undermined
When he imagined how bereft
He'd feel if he would be denied
Her love, in fear she would be spied
Upon perhaps, or just resolved
That suddenly to get involved
Was hardly worth the cost.
Yet nothing could be done but set
His mind to work at hand and let
Good sense prevail. All could be lost
Of what he'd worked for years to gain
If now he gave his heart free rein.

He turned to Leonardo and
Just nodded to the wooden box.
The work ahead and its demands
Would challenge what was orthodox.
The vanities of portraiture,
Best suited for an immature
And pampered child of noble stock
Would prove a fitting work to mock
Between themselves until this shroud
Took on the aura of the real
So palpable the Pope would kneel
And praise its power to a proud
(and generously grateful) prince.
More work would come if this convinced.

Albedo

PART III

*Innocent's illness worsening. He calls upon Franceschetto
to carry out his bidding and consolidate his power.*

As Maddalena spent her days
Now primped and posed and quietly
Seduced, her husband's wretched ways
Had waned, the dull society
Of those of Milan's demimonde
Made him suspect that those who fawned
And cooed to win his favour just
Believed affection and his trust
Would keep them safe, untouched, assured
As long as he was Innocent's
Most favoured son, beneficence,
Like ill-won fortune would endure.
He longed for their respect apart
From all that soothed his blackened heart.

Yet knowing flattery at best
Was all that he was apt to get
He opted for a little rest
Out in the country where he'd let
The healing waters of the springs

And weightless thoughts on weightless things
Move him to pitying himself,
For all the power and the wealth
That God had put within his hands
Was not enough to satisfy
Him. Now alone, he wondered why
These mendicants with outstretched hands
In all their misery still seemed
Much more at peace, with eyes that gleamed …

Suffused with faith so genuine
They seemed to pity him his lot.
He could not help but to begin
To question all he'd ever thought
About the very basis of
His father's claim to preach the love
Of Jesus to his suffering flock.
Such baseless pride, unfit to mock
The ones who truly lived the word.
He found he'd lost his appetite
To do much more than wax contrite
In notes he wrote alone, assured
That no one would be privy to
These thoughts he called "my soul's rescue".

It's hard now to imagine what
Could have occurred if he had claimed
The time to concentrate and shut
His door to Niccolo, who came
From Rome, with secret letter sealed
By Innocent, and told to yield
To no one but Cybo and place
The letter in his hands (or face
The wrath of what the Holy See
Deemed fit for one who would betray
The highest office). Unafraid,

(If willed so), calm as he could be,
The messenger Niccolo stood
Before him, smiling knight of wood.

*Poor Franceschetto. His father Innocent had some passion with his
appetites at least. He enjoyed sinning and he did it well, yet the worst
thing about Cybo is that he was more of a melancholic than he could
have ever been an interesting villain. His dissolute nature was rooted in
his frustrated sense of defeat with faith. I don't think he got any sensual
pleasure at all from the suffering and subjugation he put others through.
Perhaps he could have become a great firebrand like Savonarola if he
could only have been seized with belief, but all was negation. He did
not have the intellect of an Iago to make of his relations with others
some psychopathic exercise in playwrighting, plotting their actions and
responses from scene to scene in his mind. He found no delight or faith
in himself; his contempt was turned inward.*

*I knew so many like him, among my clientele in Italy, enchanted by
the thought of war as some spiritual salvation. Perhaps they got it, in
the end.*

"I've come with words of urgency
Regarding how your father fares.
Though not yet an emergency
It's true he's in his surgeons' care.
But what is urgent, as he states
Here in this note, is less his fate
Than what he fears once word is out
That he's unwell. The once devout
And dutiful who've long held sway
In city states and regions near
And far will start to plot a clear
Path to his office and away
From any claims that you could stake
Within this realm for your own sake."

Cybo looked him up and down
Then slowly broke into a grin,
Amused by him, his earnest frown.
He nodded for him to come in,
Then gestured to the wardrobe chair
Where he could wait, while with an air
Of grave concern he tore the seal
Then laughed, as if he could conceal
He could not comprehend the words.
He tossed it to Niccolo, then
And barked, his honour to defend,
"He knows that Latin's my preferred
Discourse, not vulgar tongue. So here,
You read. Make each word loud and clear."

Niccolo nodded, took a breath
To try and still his trembling hands,
Aware that he'd be risking death
If he should fail this curt command.
He spoke of Innocent's belief
That he had probably a brief
Time left – it could be weeks or days.
There seemed but few effective ways
The doctors knew to stop the blood
That came when he would cough at night
And all the strength he had to fight
The constant plotting and the flood
Of pagan influences in
The Empire now was wearing thin.

He knew that Leonardo was
Entrusted with a stratagem.
"Lorenzo chose him just because
For decades he'd clung to the hem
Of every Florentine brocade
That the Medici house had made,

His loyalty a prudent choice,
Assuring none would ever voice
What men of cloth had known since he
Was once arrested as a boy:
That it was well-known he enjoys
The Florentine fraternity's
Particular pursuits – and worse
Touts the Lucretian universe.

"All this is known, I've been aware
For years, yet I have looked away
So no one could say that I cared
For what posterity will say
Alone, that I could see the gains
In charting heresy's domain,
My path ensured a straighter course
Onto the route the saints endorse
To build the city Augustine
Believed could be the world entire.
This, I maintain, we should aspire
To, yet if his work should demean
Our higher aims, you'll be compelled
To find the crime to which he held."

At this, Cybo had raised his hand
For Niccolo to stop. He turned
And paced, now like a horse unmanned
With thoughts of heretics that burned
At stakes he'd proudly ordered set
Ablaze in campaigns past, and yet
He couldn't help but feel that now
There was a desperate tone to how
His father justified his claim
To some imperial design
While here, with so much undefined
About the future, just his name

And feeble legacy was all
He cared about before the fall.

And whether that would come before
His health grew worse seemed moot at best.
The Curia was at its core
Corrupted, and the self-confessed
Reluctant acolytes who'd paid
Their one indulgence to be made
One washed of sin, infused with love,
The Lord their God, unmoved above,
Would now be poised to take their wealth
And influence throughout the states
And regions loyal to the weight
And force of history (with cries yet quelled
For freedom from the peasant's yoke),
And turn to one whose fears they stoked.

All this he ruminated on
Aloud while Niccolo observed.
Perhaps Cybo thought he'd withdrawn
From listening and had reserved
All comment out of due respect,
Yet once he paused he could detect
The boy's apparent need to speak.
So, more amused than in some pique
Provoked by this effrontery,
He smiled and said, "But what would you,
In all your wisdom say? Your view's
As valid, so be blunt with me."
Niccolo smiled, unsure about
How safe this was, yet truth will out.

One evening, after more than a few glasses of wine, Farrell told me of
his time as a young priest. It was less a calling than what was expected

from large, poor families in Dublin; the brightest boy was "given" to the Church, sent to the O'Connell school run by the Christian Brothers. And yes, as you can imagine, the monitors and the priests themselves initiated Farrell into the rites they kept hidden from the congregation. Yet his intellect offered him a route of escape. He had won a scholarship to All Souls where he studied the history of art and "learned too much to go back to miserable old Dublin and become some milquetoast of a parish priest, corrupting innocents, as I was corrupted, and suffering far too little for it."

Yet once he was out of the Church he had a hard time of it. He was going to write, perhaps make a living as a journalist, but all that was on offer was a position reviewing films for the Irish Independent, *where he distinguished himself for his inability to meet deadlines and by his drinking on the job. He barely lasted six months.*

It was Bernard Delegarde who saved him. He had taught Farrell at the O'Connell school and they had kept up a correspondence over the years. He, too, was an outsider who felt the Vatican was corrupt to the core, yet the Church was all he knew. He believed that he could work to save it from within. When Farrell arrived in Rome to take on an archivist's position within the Vatican Library, Delegarde had housed him, fed him, got him gradually sober and functioning again. Later, when this mentor and saviour had come to Farrell for help, how could he possibly say no?

On a night when he had invited Antony and me to his apartment to have dinner, I asked Delegarde about all this when Farrell had gone to piss. Delegarde was a big, burly man, with hands like a boxer's. He just smiled and said, in that musical lilt. "Now do you really believe I would ever be that kind-hearted a fellow?"

"It's my belief, though let me say
I disagree about your point
That my word is in any way
As valid; no one will anoint
Me with the power to comprehend
All that your future will depend

Upon. Still, all that humbly said,
I sense your father's been misled,
If that is any comfort for
You as you feel compelled to heed
His words – and yet I must concede
Despite theatrics, at its core
There is some wisdom to this course
Of action – a display of force."

Cybo could not restrain his laugh.
"Some wisdom, yes? And from your vast
Experience in such statecraft,
The lessons that you've drawn from past
Inducements to incite a state
Of fear among the poor, whose fate
Is miserable enough without
Some baseless charge that cause for doubt
In Rome's entrustment with their faith
Is proof that they're in Satan's thrall,
You think that answering this call
To arms ensures I'd be unscathed
From what is fated to ensue
When this reign ends and gets its due?"

"It's true that fortune's wheel cannot
Be somehow turned the other way
In motion, and a counterplot
Could mean, for those who would betray
Your father that you drew the line
Of battle they left undefined
And so compelled them to react,
Yet this does not at root detract
From what remains the wisest course
Of action; it's an argument
To steel the many who resent
The power you have. A show of force

That you initiate before
Your father's death will help you more.

"Your welfare and survival past
The day of his demise should be
Your sole concern, no scrap will last
Of his regime, but those who see
In you a force unto yourself
With faithful allies, power and wealth
Will find cause to reflect upon
The risks of battle and how strong
Alliances they cultivate
Will be as constant as they claim
If word of numbers that you'd slain
Spread to their subjects, whose bleak fate –
The first in battle to advance –
Believe they'd have but little chance."

Cybo could not conceal his shock
As Niccolo unconsciously
Began to gesture as he talked
To state his case more forcefully
As if the yawning chasm that
Had split their worlds by who begat
Them now had just begun to close.
Who taught this whelp all that he knows
Of statecraft and the workings of
The court and all its subtle codes?
The wisdom that so freely flowed
Within the darkened music of
His coarse declarative attempts
At counsel pierced Cybo's contempt.

"I'm not sure why I feel I can
Confide in you – I fear I've been
Up here for far too long a span

Of time, now changed by what I've seen
Of those whose faith is more profound
Than what I've known. I've ceded ground
That I will soon regret, perhaps
Yet old delusions set the traps
That snare the man who can't perceive
At root survival must transcend
Some sacrifice for others' ends,
That fate dictates what we believe.
To act for oneself's always just.
At root, it's all that I can trust."

Niccolo wasn't sure if now
Was time to nod or interject,
Enthused enough to tell him how
Like many, he could not detect
If he had wisdom of his own
Or if, because he was the lone
Inheritor of all the Pope
Could call upon and even hope
From sense of duty would endure,
Yet it was clear he knew his mind
Was hardly one who'd be defined
By family name, that was assured.
There wasn't more that he could say;
Alas, Cybo would go his way.

"Whatever doubts that I may feel
About the wisdom of this dark
Campaign to force the poor to kneel
In fear, my role is to embark
Upon this wretched course and show,
When rival factions come to blows
To claim control of this empire
That no upstart who would aspire
To take that crumbling throne of ghosts

Can entertain thoughts of success
Without seducing me to bless,
Aid and abet from some outpost
Far from the fray, enriched, well-armed,
A force unchallenged – and unharmed."

With this, he took the letter and
Held it above a candle flame.
The paper shriveled in his hand
Consumed, just as his father's name
Would be now by his rivals' zeal
To claim his throne but still conceal
All machinations from the eyes
Of the devout, soothed by the lies
Of those who'd rule the Holy See.
"I thank you, you can leave me now
To plot my course." Niccolo bowed
And made his exit silently,
Unseen, now that the moon had scaled
The clouds and darkness dropped her veil.

Albedo

PART IV

The seduction of Andalus.

The heavy heat of summer now
Bore down upon the valley of
The Po, and who would not allow
These languid days to bend to love's
Awakenings? No slumber in
The afternoons atoned for sins
Of restless nights with fevered dreams
From too much wine drunk while one schemes
To make seduction effortless
Despite constraints of time and place,
Realities one best not face
For how could one at all address
The fact that all these hours alone
Might turn desire as cold as stone?

To think, within this silence, while
She sat in place, so calm and still,
She'd glance at him and start to smile
Assuring him they shared the will;
He only had to find the way,
While Leonardo spent each day

Now lost to what had seemed at first
A daub upon a rag, at worst
An exercise to see if this
Strange little box was any use.
No more – he quietly excused
Himself each morning with a kiss
Upon her hand, apologized.
His work was for her father's eyes.

In the first year after the war Olivia had come to stay with me in a villa I had rented in Spoleto. She had just left Cambridge and had her first paid acting role as Desdemona with the RSC; she had arrived in Rome because her new agent told her that a man named De Sica was auditioning English actors at Cinecitta. It was that summer that I told her of Ocular.

At first she found my subject and all that I had written quite strange. She viewed the Vatican and those affiliated with it as about as relevant and worthy of consideration as radio comedies and football. Farrell had joined us at the villa for a few days, and she could barely tolerate this odd Irishman who had the air of one of those failed bohemians who hung around the lobbies at opening night parties in London. That Farrell was working at the Vatican was indicative of how louche and decadent that world really was at its core, she said. It made her think the Communists might be right about the perverts and homosexuals having taken the church over for years. She would murmur to herself when Farrell would come down to breakfasts in his wrinkled tennis shirts and shiny old suit pants, smelling of Turkish tobacco. Always had his nose in some ancient book, like one of our father's old friends.

How she came to despise her younger self for all this. She told me, when we were both middle-aged, that she was just a spoiled, self-centered child who knew nothing of the world when she had come to Rome. I did not disagree.

The only way she could lash out at me at the time for betraying our shared innocence – yes, we were that kind of family – was in her criticism of what I had written. From the very beginning she was cold

on it, thought it revealed that all I cared about was power and the
machinations of men to subjugate everything to their will.

I took her criticism seriously. How could I not? This scene was my
response to it.

She gladly granted him his leave
Revealing not a moment's thought
She gave to it, for she believed
Each moment with Andalus ought
To be considered as a gift
And yet her thoughts would often drift
To what required such secrecy,
So now alone, an urge to see
His work in progress seemed an apt
Inducement to the moment's rest
Andalus hardly could suggest,
So focussed was he, so enrapt
With what he finally could do
To show his art and love were true.

And yet this portrait mattered less
To her. She now yearned for the proof
Of what he once wrote and confessed
Before he turned so cool, aloof
And yes, subservient to the will
Of Leonardo. Was he still
The man who promised her much more?
It fell to her, before he bored
Her half to death to break the glass
That seemed to trap the air they breathed.
With just a few words, she believed
This awkwardness would fade at last.
She turned to him and smiled, then said,
"This heat is going to my head."
He started, as if woken from

A hazy dream his brush made true
To life, and she just smiled, said, "Come
Attend me, what harm could it do?
I need some water and a rest.
I trust in you to know where's best
To lay my head in darkness for
A while in peace – and with a door
That locks so no one could surprise
Us, if you know what that could mean.
Some moments should remain unseen,
Except perhaps, for just your eyes."
He smiled, for he could tell where she
Had fantasized their tryst would be.

"You know that Leonardo would
Consider it a grave betrayal.
The trust he now has placed in me could
All be lost if we should fail
To make of all the work within
That box an image real as sin."
She laughed at this. "What sin would you
Consider real? Among the few
Days he's appeared, it seems his eye
Is solely trained on you. If there's
A sin original in where he stares
And what he's sculpted, from what I
Presume you modeled for, then yes,
His soul is lost, as they suggest."

*What became clear to me, the more I thought through this process of
the image trapped within the camera obscura, was the amount of time
required for it to "take" on treated fabric. One could have someone pose
for hours, or one could simply place a subject at the required angle and
distance, given the power of the lens and the mechanism of the iris over
a period of days.*

Antony explained it to me; it was mostly his conception. He had worked it out in such detail, down to the days it would have taken, given the chemical composition of this primitive version of photographic paper and the hours of natural light. He sketched it all out for me one morning in the library, said he'd had it rattling around his brain for years. I think at one point, back at All Souls, he had hoped to publish a paper on all of this, and then of course he got word that some old friends were interested in having him come to the Vatican. So ended his aspirations for a life in academia. As I watched him write so fast, as if he was at a séance, possessed by some spirit, I understood why his friends in Rome considered him so valuable.

In the writing of Ocular *I wanted to make more of the contrast between how the painting of Maddalena slowly emerged from thousands of decisions on the canvas, so patiently arrived upon day after day, and how the image on the shroud just developed once the materials and the machine for image-making were prepared. I think I had hoped to investigate the paradoxes and correspondences that were inherent in these two very different approaches to creating the aura of the real. Such matters kept Antony and me talking. It was all a kind of sportive diversion from the real world, I know, but by that point what had serving the real world done for either of us, really?*

Once I completed Ocular *I realized I had a mind that worked more like Antony Farrell's. I had outgrown my "lyrical tendencies," all the preciousness and self-regard of my younger years. Thank God all that was over. This realization led me to more than three decades of working for scholarly credibility, and of course the self-publishing of* The Camera and the Photograph: Da Vinci's Shroud.

It should have been Antony's book, but by the time of its publication he had long abandoned such interests, just as he had so abruptly abandoned his career in Rome. If Antony was intellectually engaged, he would work obsessively, as if it were all that mattered, but as soon as he lost faith in or respect for those who required his services, he could disappear for weeks.

I managed to get him a position at Vidler's in London when I heard he was struggling – this would have been just a few years after he had helped arrange Tomassoni's exhibition in Dublin. Connie realized how brilliant he was and was grooming him to be a director. How I would have loved the same to happen to me, but I was marked early on as just my father's boy, too superficial and prone to bad company. With Antony, Connie could quickly tell he had such an eye, and not just with Renaissance painting. Antony once gave me a monograph on Turner that he was working on during those years and it was like nothing I had ever read before, just brilliant, but I don't believe he ever finished it. Maybe all of this was owing to his wrestling with his demons; I don't know. He was very secretive. I knew by then he had spent some time in Tangiers and had fallen in with some shady characters. When he returned, he could have been addicted to heroin once again; no one out of the London office was absolutely sure. By around '65 or '66 he had used up all the good will Connie could afford him. He left for America and I lost touch with him. He lost touch with everyone, really. Such promise gone to waste.

I got a postcard from him around '75 or '76 from Nicaragua, of all places. He said he had ended up in Boston, working at some mission through one of his old friends in what he called his Irish Vatican mafia, "the gang that really knew how to make crime pay". He was down there mixing with Somoza's pals, it seems, "doing God's work". It was there he died.

"You mean this figure he has done?
It's just so what is trapped inside
Will take, providing that the sun
Will bare its rays. If he had tried
To sculpt my likeness, you should know
I don't have to disrobe to show
You I could not claim that physique.
If anyone, that figure speaks
Of Leonardo working from
The mirror in his study. His
Own method to obscure, dismiss
Those who'd believe his best work comes
From looking only deep within
Himself – the glass conceals his grin."

She rose from where she sat and took
His hand, then put a finger to
His lips. "Words best belong in books,
Not now, between us, where what's true
Does not require such subtle turns
Of phrase. But only here, what burns
Within your heart, revealed by touch
Is all I need to know. Too much
Of art constrains a man's desire.
That's all you have to learn from him.
Your master's tempests should not trim
Your sails, what seems a distant fire
Of promise in your skies is just
His play of light, his darkened lust."

With that, she led him over to
The camera, then placed a kiss
Upon his lips, said, "What would you
Suggest that we might do in this
That could compare as a profound
Experience, where we'd have grounds
To claim a great creative act
Occurred within this box? The fact
We both must keep in mind is that
We can't be sure we'll ever see
Each other after this, I'll be
Returned to Florence, to get fat
And ugly through my married years.
So give me reason for my tears."

For once, Andalus did not feel
He had to question how he felt
For here were all her charms revealed.
No altar where he'd bowed and knelt
Could summon his devotion now
With greater force; he knew that how

Her portrait would take on that stark
Mysterious power that bore the mark
Of deeper vision would require
A greater sacrifice, a claim
Upon his heart that wealth or fame
Could hardly stake, that his desire
Was in the end his greater guide –
If now exposed – no place to hide.

And as the camera's door had closed
The curtains at the windows stirred
With just the faintest breeze. A rose
He'd plucked for her that she, demure,
Had placed within a drinking glass
Upon the ledge, now turned its last
Few petals to bathe in the sun's warm rays.
Each fell, she'd said, to mark the days
That they had spent alone. And though
She wouldn't even risk a glance
Upon his work, this one great chance
That he had waited for to show
His talent to the world, she knew
What he now coloured would be true.

Citrinitas

PART I

*Franceschetto declares his bankruptcy and debt. He appeals
to Lorenzo for his rescue and for funding of the campaign he must
embark on in his father's name.*

The one diversion that remained
Of interest to Lorenzo through
These days where obligation chained
Him to the desk, as he reviewed
The drafts of each agreement signed
With Sforza that had redefined
All aspects of their new compact,
Expressed in terms succinct, exact
So bloodlessly transformed here by
The alchemy of legalese,
Was falconry, his sole release
That got him far from all who'd eye
His every move within Milan.
Out in the wood, his days began.

He called his bird Lucretius for
It seemed he could, just like the wise
Old Roman let his focus bore
So deeply through what human eyes

Accepted as the world appeared,
The surface plane that all adhered
To, all believed in to be real,
While custom served to block, conceal
The deeper vision where the true
Design and inner workings of
All as below, and so above
Would come into majestic view,
The falcon soared and found its prey
As winged proof this view held sway.

The references to Lucretius came out of a conversation Farrell and I had one evening, early in our friendship. We had spent most of the spring of '43 avoiding the inevitable conversations about how the war was actually going to end for the simple reason that defeat for Britain seemed inevitable.

Yet Farrell insisted, based on what he had heard from Delegarde, that there was something to all these rumours about a Manhattan project, and that a bomb of incredible power was almost a reality. Farrell was assured it would change everything.

I remember how skeptical I was. Everybody wished for some secret weapon, some touch of magic that would save us. All talk of the wonders of the atom and what these scientists were working on had the cheap aura of science fiction about it. Such a dramatic turn of fate couldn't really be credible. I think it offended me aesthetically. Reality could not work like bad art — but of course it does.

No doubt it was in an effort to raise the tone that Farrell started blathering on about Lucretius. The Roman poet had been there first with all this talk of atoms centuries ago. Farrell explained that his long poem On The Nature of Things *was central to the secret, radical pagan vision Lorenzo and his little cabal of thinkers adopted and adhered to, in opposition to the mechanistic, medieval understanding of the universe enforced by the Holy See. I looked it up myself and, as usual, Farrell was right:*

"I'll now proceed to argument and proof
Of what makes up the soul, and what its substance.
To begin, I say the soul is subtly built
Of infinitesimal atoms. You may see
And learn that this is so from what's to come ...

This fact, too, tells the nature of the soul,
How fine its fabric, and in how small a space
It could be held, if it were all rolled up ..."

I liked that: the soul trapped in fine fabric. It seemed exactly right for
Ocular. In Lucretius went.

Yet jessed and tethered to the taut
And fitted gauntlet with a hood
That kept him blinded, not a thought
Or memory of flight through wood
And field could stir Lucretius from
A state of eerie calm. Like some
Austerely sculpted statue that
Had now been brought to life he sat,
The force of life within him coiled
So tightly that Lorenzo sensed
The falcon's strength if he had tensed
A muscle. Then, his slumber spoiled,
He ruffled, like an archer's quill
His arrowed plumage, poised to kill.

Lorenzo thought that, if he spoke
Of how Lucretius made him muse
On nature's mysteries, some joke
Or jibe at him, less to amuse
Than prick him for his haughty air
Would be Cybo's response. He'd care
But little, yet this was his son-
In-law, who had, it seemed, begun

To curiously seek him out,
Accompany him at this hour
And intimate that papal power
Was what he was concerned about,
That it was in their interests to
Make of their bond a strength renewed.

He played the student well-behaved,
Who hoped to learn in falconry
An ancient art the noble saved
From all the usual pedantry,
Which only gave Lorenzo pause
To wonder to himself what caused
This sudden, suspect change in him,
Like candlelight glimpsed down a dim
And long-abandoned corridor.
A flicker of intelligence
Was too remote still to convince
Him there was not a motive for
This sober, soldierly respect
With no false smiles he could detect.

He let this new charade play out
Until the moon was full again
Whatever this was all about
A spirit like Cybo's could feign
Such rectitude for just so long
Before what still remained so strong
Within his nature would return,
That slender candle lit would burn,
Night's flickering, waxen effigy,
And gutter out before the dawn
Returning him, with drunken yawn
Back to the slumber of his free
And easy ways, his humour fixed;
A nobler taint would not be mixed.

And yet the moon glowed in its full
Dimension, lighting up the sky.
Temptation had not seemed to dull
Cybo's resolve at dawn's reply.
With one of Sforza's falcons lent
And poised upon his arm he meant
To be Lorenzo's model, proud,
A form so decorous, avowed
To show the measure of his worth
Should he be watched. Appraised by no
One but himself, he seemed to throw
His chest out, mime how, with his girth,
Nobility assumes its true
Dominion and receives its due.

Lorenzo couldn't help but drop
A measure of his guard despite
Himself and ask what made him stop
So suddenly from taking night's
Embrace of darkness as his own
Here in Milan, adopt this tone
Of something like humility
And poise; this new civility,
Though welcome on its face was such
A sudden change, so unprovoked
There had to be a motive cloaked
In some resolve he'd thought too much
Upon, then stitched with guilt to form
A figure to constrain his scorn.

At this Cybo could not but smile
At last, concede there might be truth
In that, "yet time alone here, while
Imposed, let me think on my youth
And realize, despite what I
Had once thought fit to flout, deny

As truly meaningful, I've come
To see the greater wisdom from
The sage words fit to guide his reign.
There's deeper understanding of
The failings of a father's love
And how one rages yet in vain
In verses from a simple play
Than all I'd ever heard him say."

Lorenzo beamed, he couldn't hide
Despite himself, how such thoughts charmed
Him, filled him with a sense of pride,
Made him at once contrite, disarmed.
He'd been so harsh, dismissive, when
He'd heard Cybo had left to spend
Some time alone in thought and prayer,
Presumed he'd never learn to care
About such deeper questions posed
In hours of silence, with the words
Upon the pages long referred
To as " those pagan myths," exposed
As dangerous by poets wise
Enough to spout the safest lies.

"You sound as if you've come to face
What life alone must bring you to.
No trust in God's eternal grace
Consoles the heart that yearns for true
Connection to the greater source
Of wisdom, with its primal force
That surges through a noble soul
And won't cease 'til it makes one whole."
Lucretius stirred upon his wrist
As he, despite himself, could not
Remain composed in quiet thought
But realized he'd made a fist,

A gesture that betrayed the fight
Within him, sure that he was right.

"That all seems true to me, and yet
What you call life alone I would
Just qualify, with some regret;
Necessity might be a good
Approximation of the cause
That led me to discern these flaws
Within this soul's averred design.
If ash and lead can be refined
Revealing silver to be found
Within the hearth once it has cooled
Then maybe I have not been fooled
By allegories deemed unsound
And dangerous to propagate,
The proof obtains, confounds the fates."

Their horses slowly trotted through
The wood. The sun in dappled rays
Now tinged the distant shades of blue
In dawn's approaching golden haze.
It came on with a sudden hush,
Their path at once appeared so lush
And fragrant from the summer's last
Upsurge of life, now fading fast.
Lorenzo, prone to moments where
It seemed that beauty's hand could reach
Into his heart and steal his speech
Just nodded with a priestly air,
Anticipating that a kind
Of soul's reprieve was on his mind.

"Explain to me just what you mean
When you speak of necessity.
It seems a shade now haunts unseen

Your waking hours. Such gravity
Is better worn when you have aged
And found that all that one has raged
Against in younger days recedes
Upon a distant plane; you're freed
From those imperatives that surge
Within the blood from appetites
And fears of emptiness, despite
The constant feast of life; no purge
Can serve to purify and cleanse
Until time shapes the means – and ends."

"A man is the room he is in." So says the Japanese proverb. If so, then this cottage with its one shelf of books, three Ranuccio Tomassoni paintings, and about fifty bottles of wine left in the cellar, may set the terms by which I can finally define myself.

I find it interesting that as a young man I had given these words to Lorenzo, the ultimate Machiavellian. To conceal the passions, especially the darkest or most illicit, only to savour the eventual consummation of desire or taste of revenge, was a justification for my own inaction over the years. Yet very little of a younger man's sensuality has stayed with me.

I still tell myself I have distilled my pleasures down to essentials. I look back with a sense of relief that most of my passions have deserted me. Like a gambler who realizes he has no money left, I don't have the resources to fuel my self-loathing anymore.

Cybo could only cast his gaze
Upon the narrow path before
He spoke; the pride that he was raised
With seared his blunt words to the core
Within him, molten, glowing red.
No safe return from all he'd said
Could now be made. He had to take
This route he'd chosen, not forsake

What he believed was truly wise.
If he was to survive the years
Ahead, he had to hide his fears,
Yet too much truth suffused his lies.
With all this conversation cost
Him, now he felt his courage lost.

He swallowed deep, and then at last
He uttered what he had rehearsed
To vault free of his father's past
And all that he had been so cursed
To call his family's legacy.
"My creditors view secrecy
As sadly wise, essential to
The mutual trust a chosen few
Among their friends can be assured
Of, as they try to make each date
For payment that they owe, sums great
Or small. They say I am ensured
Discretion won't be compromised,
Regardless of how ill-advised.

"For no amount of trust could serve
To make of one compelled to spend
More than a king of fools deserved.
I know I'm not one you should lend
A fortune to. My sirens called
To me of course, ensured the fall
From grace, my wreckage on the rocks
Of debt; yet I was one who mocked
Such servitude to vice as proof
That those of humble birth were chained
Like galley slaves to pre-ordained
Damnation that set sail in youth
To languish in those latitudes
For years, with rage unspent, subdued.

"Now here I am, enslaved as well
Despite my soul's awakening
To how my craft is bound for hell.
There's really no escape; it brings
Me to an end predicted for
A prodigal, and yet there's more
I must accomplish as a son
And heir. I've really just begun
To serve some greater cause than the
Debasement of my appetites.
To finally learn what's true and right,
Consoling as it is, leaves me
In hardly any better state
When I'm consigned this debtor's fate."

Lorenzo looked upon the hood
That kept Lucretius still and blind
And suddenly he understood
What Franceschetto hoped to find
In him, the one who would rescue
Him from the debts he owed. Virtue
Discovered and proclaimed was not
As frankly credible as what
Could be revealed from word to deed.
Just as the hood subdued, this act
Was meant to blind him from the fact
There was at hand an urgent need.
And yet, there hardly seemed a way
To solve this if he didn't pay.

"You understand I'm well aware
When words are chosen to seduce,
For in my youth I tried my share
Of subterfuges to produce
From all the fragile pieces of
Some broken unrequited love

Or vessel of ambition I'd
Let shatter or, ill-starred, collide
With one that had the most wind in
Its sails. I spoke as one concerned
With nothing more than what was learned
From sounding to the depths of sin
The measure of my humble soul,
I knew the acts and played my role."

Here I know I let this metaphor pivot from one image to another, pulling the thread of meaning taut enough that it risks snapping (if I can coin yet another metaphor). But ambition was so central to this work I was constantly examining it, it seems.

There is something about this whole stanza that reads like a perfect epitaph for the battle I briefly fought for some literary credibility – and lost.

"But know you really didn't need
To go to such great lengths to pry
The princely sum that will have freed
You from the need to live a lie.
My daughter's state of innocence
Concerns me most. Take no offence;
I'm sure there's much in what you've said
That's from the heart and not the head
For deeper truths remain the source
That nurtures every stratagem;
Yet both of us clutch to the hem
Of honour's robe, and so of course
If only for appearance sake
I'll pay what now keeps you awake."

Cybo knew that he could only nod
With deference and feigned respect.
Regardless of how much a fraud

He knew Lorenzo could detect
He was, this state of servitude
Demanded he remain subdued
And play this scene until its end,
Which meant, of course, some hours to spend
Still posed upon this horse, yet now
Less like a falcon than a finch
With eyes that can't stay on one inch
Of ground for seconds or allow
A thought to form beyond a need
His old impulses could be freed.

Perhaps he really would attend
To debts his creditors had deemed
Untenable, yet he could spend
For his own private force what seemed
Impossible just days before.
And this was necessary, more
Than mollifying all but just
The ones he rightly feared, who must
Be dealt with or incur their wrath,
With forces of their own and no
Concern for who'd become their foe,
This bastard son. The shaded path
To claim the power that he craved
Had now been cleared, his honour saved.

Lorenzo smiled and gestured to
Cybo as if to wave him on.
"I know that you have much to do
Now that we've talked, another long
And tiresome morning spent with me,
Compelled to listen and to be
As interested in all I care
About, as if we really shared
Some greater bond than vows you took

To make our families as one.
Just let me speak to you as son
And heir then, when I say don't look
Upon your presence as required.
Consider yours what you desire."

There wasn't more Cybo could do
But make as if, upon his feet
His nod would be a bow, as true
As he could make this quick retreat.
His wounded pride was more sincere
Than he intended, and he feared
The longer that he tarried now
The more he'd later ponder how
He let himself be so demeaned;
So, scarcely noticing the bird
Upon his arm, without a word
He galloped off, as if he'd seen
Just like Lucretius, far away
His innocent, unknowing prey.

Interlude: The Proof

She rises, well before the angry sun
That in this fateful summer's final days
Insists, before this portrait's all but done
To bear down on Milan its scorching rays
Increasing what is now her fevered state,
What she attributed at first to love –
Though since it all has worsened as of late –
Believes this sickness is a portent of
The proof that forms a life all of its own
And makes a mother of a lovesick girl;
The lover's pliant poses turn to stone,
Arms stretched to hold the weight of this new world.
She takes a breath, collects herself, her fears
Of all-this-means-now bringing her to tears.

Dissimulation will not serve to make
Of this a sudden, but acclaimed surprise
For only on her nuptials did she break
Her chaste resolve with him, whom she's despised
Since well before she wore this wedding ring;
There is no telling what he'll do to her
Or what his surge of unchecked rage will bring
Upon her family so he's assured
Of his revenge, his honour deemed restored.
No longer as a mother could she be
Considered worthy, and to play the whore
Was all but an impossibility.
She and her child would perish at his hands;
To save herself is what her state demands.

Out of all the thematic variations on proof, Maddalena's pregnancy is the hinge moment that turns the plot, drives the momentum of the final five scenes. From the static, frieze-like scenography of the early part of the work to the crosscutting that occurs later on, I wanted to make this brief discovery scene the moment of stillness that marks a final transition.

I was no playwright – at least I was not consciously aware of my dramaturgy; yet I did see many of these scenes play out in my head as if they were on stage, a kind of black box in my mind, one stripped of all artifice, save for the characters and the language. It was years later, back in London when I was running with that crowd that drank at Muriel's, when I first saw, in his magnificent, filthy mess of a studio, Bacon's paintings of Pope Innocent X and thought to myself: yes, there it is. These are the theatrics I had aspired to with Ocular Proof. *Aspired to, rather than achieved.*

Citrinitas

PART II

*Leonardo visits Gethsemane and appeals for her help in
the creation of the shroud.*

The time when Leonardo could
Allow himself to put his trust
In all Andalus understood
Of alchemy had passed; he just
Could not abide the meagre gains
Of trial and error, all the pains
Of labouring with elements
Unstable, and the arguments
Of some hieratic code of laws
One had to take on faith, it seemed,
With all the logic of a dream.
The "opus" stripped effect from cause
And gave of time by lunar phase
Such primacy – much else erased.

And so, frustrated, he resolved
To speak with her alone, for she
Appeared to know what was involved
To make of ancient alchemy
More than an act occult, profane
But work where something real obtained.

He set off for those narrow streets
He knew too well, for there he'd meet
From time to time the ones who'd serve
His needs, investigations in
Anatomies and carnal sin,
Where, with a gaze that would not swerve
From proof both church and state forbade,
He would not flinch from any blade.

The "opus": a real term. In fact the original "magnum opus" was the work done on the self, how one could be transformed or "purified" out of the base mixture of elements and influences to a being fully realized.

This was Farrell's idea here. Perhaps he was a hippie before his time; he loved this kind of nonsense. He spoke to me of heading to Cairo when the war was finally over. He was going to take with him the writings of Hermes Trismegistus. He had his languages so he presumed he could get a position at the National Library there and work on a monograph about alchemy in the era of the Caliphate, while he "experimented" with his own version of transformation.

The truth I learned later was that Farrell, like Harry Maes and Fabrizio Longhi, was probably a heroin addict even then. He justified it by saying he believed the body was a kind of laboratory for the experience of altered states, and heroin offered a compelling version of transcendence during the bleak months at the end of the war. North Africa would allow him to indulge himself with heroin cheaply, without any real worry about the police.

When he returned, he seemed changed. He was more detached, and he had a strange glare, as if he was suddenly self-conscious about looking me in the eye and so had to lock his gaze there, just to prove he was not being evasive. It was the beginning of me gradually distancing myself. I didn't feel like I really knew him anymore.

Gethsemane in truth had long
Expected him, for how could such
A process where no single wrong

Step could be made, and where so much
Depended on what books could not
Provide, the trust that no forethought
Of method and its dry report
Could substitute for the retort
And careful tending to the flame,
As transmutations carried out,
Within that dance of faith and doubt,
Ever find their form without the frame
Of mind emboldened by these rites,
Forbidden, carried out by night?

For didn't he, from all she heard
Not seem to live two lives? One for
His patron's favours, all conferred
For work that surely had to bore
Him past the point of caring but
For how much he could claim his cut,
Enabling him to, in those hours
Most men devoted to what flowers
Within that humble garden, home
And hearth. His restless mind and heart
Was less enrapt with making art
Than taking from these ancient tomes
That wedded one to wisdom not
A word for granted – or forgot.

It really was a brilliant, intuitive decision of MI6's top brass to look
to men like Farrell and me for espionage. Playing the spy allowed me
to transmute all my feelings of shame about never fitting in, never
completing the project of assimilation, despite my parents' expectations.
By working for MI6 (yet still not one of them or accepted – how
brilliant on their part to realize I would be more effective that way),
I could tell myself I was attuned to a world of greater ideals, higher
virtues. As for Farrell, with such deep reserves of Irish Catholic guilt, he

took to the plan of creating these forgeries of paintings – as the Vatican's bargaining chips with the Nazis – with a quiet fervor I will always admire.

Yet I was really like an actor in an amateur troupe compared to Antony. I could read the script, mouth all the right words and carry out my work conscientiously but Farrell could go at it all with a deeper sense of commitment. He was the professional. He read the angles of everything more completely, and he could think further steps ahead. I'm sure that when he had met with his MI6 contact in Rome in that windowless office that smelled of old books and wet raincoats, the plan for the forgeries was nothing more than a notion, pitched to him as a way to draw out the Curia's loyalties and bind them to the Allied cause. It was he who made it real, like a builder who, over time, effectively becomes the architect.

He took me on his visits to the painters involved in this project. I expected him to tell them absolutely nothing of those they were painting these counterfeit works for, but he didn't seem to care. If anything, I believe he presumed that if they knew they were devoting all their time and energy to works for the Curia, they would be more motivated to come up with exceptional paintings.

I cannot say how it worked for all of the painters employed in this project. I can only speak to what I saw with Ranuccio. He could not have been more than fifteen or sixteen when he was discovered by Father Michaele at the Church of Santa Bibiana in Rome. His parents had sent him to train as a cook in the kitchen of his uncle's tavern, and in his free hours, penniless and friendless, he began to wander the streets. He told Father Michaele he had watched an Englishman sketch on the Spanish Steps and simply decided he would teach himself to do that. In less than a year the boy began to paint reproductions of the Vatican's collection and donate them to Santa Bibiana.

Farrell and I both developed an interest in his work early on. We often went out to check on the progress of the Caravaggio he was work-ing on: The Deposition from the Cross. *The boy had fashioned that studio at the back of a mechanic's garage, and Farrell and I would walk over there in the mornings or late evenings to see him paint by the light of four or five candles. We'd bring him American cigarettes and Swiss chocolate.*

Aside from a reluctant nod and mumbled thank you at the sight of the cigarettes and chocolate, Ranuccio did not react well to this. In his innocence, with all the earnestness of an altar boy who has discovered his new vocation, he struck me as if he had been born in another time.

The Deposition, *along with six other works being painted by artists we had come into contact with through Harry Maes, was among the first selections of work the Curia commissioned. If they were satisfied with the results, there was talk of as many as fifty paintings being replicated, with the originals sent to St. Mary's Cathedral in Dublin.*

From there they would be shipped out to Jack Canetti's estate near Killaloe in County Clare (Canetti was an American who worked for the Guggenheims until he made himself a quiet fortune selling work he'd smuggled out of Europe, "going freelance"). Jack had the space – an old ballroom – and he knew how to treat these paintings so they would not be damaged in storage. He also knew how to get them out of Ireland and over to America if need be. It was all well thought out and expertly managed, in large part by Farrell.

Yet Canetti was never freelance, of course. He was O.S.S. You could tell by the way he dressed – grey flannel and starched white shirts, the signet ring from Yale (he said he graduated with a mathematics degree yet he changed the subject when I asked him who his professors were), his impeccable, unaccented Berlitz Italian and the odd, center part in his pomaded hair (the one trait that betrayed him, made him look like some bartender in a speakeasy rather than an Ivy League boy and confidante of Peggy Guggenheim). The manor out in Killaloe may have been his base but he was rarely there. In the years after the war I frequently saw him with Clement Greenberg when they were involved in some exhibition in Paris or Amsterdam or Berlin of new American painting. Canetti may have been selling everything from Braque's little sketches to some of Cezanne's masterpieces back in the States, but on the other side of the ocean he operated like one of those poker faced nonentities from Eisenhower's War Department.

Some months ago I took a day trip out to the old Killaloe manor. The place was on the market for a couple of million pounds (it sold eventually to a pop star who looked like a panto pirate). I walked through the old ballroom,

with its waxed floorboards the colour of honey, and I must have stared
for a quarter of an hour up at the putti and the celestial scene of Mary
being received by the angels that was painted on the domed ceiling. They
were Canetti's touch; the work was done in the sixties.

Canetti was the only one who really knew the full extent of Farrell's
work in the Vatican, and he was also the one who made sure Farrell
was looked after when he moved to America. They got along because they
were both boys their parents gave to the church to become priests, and
they both had strayed from their vocations.

But back to Gethsemane:

She greeted Leonardo with cold
Disdain, yet hardly could conceal
A searching look, for she'd been told
So much about him that the real
Man had to measure to the frame
That fixed this image, so defamed
By those that he'd supplanted here
For Sforza's favour, and his queer
Preoccupations with these dark
Designs no patron who, allied
With Rome would sanction or provide
Unqualified support; it marked
Him as, for better or for worse,
The heretic they'd target first.

For she had seen and heard enough
Of recent gestures, shifts in tone
Among the few who'd never bluff
With threats, assured the Papal throne
Would permit all that was required
To feed the flames upon the pyres
They set alight in every town
With those they tried for show, then found
To be the worst examples of
The way a darkness roils below

Such placid waters, those one knows
Whose lips deceive, who speak of love
But are the "devil's harlots," led
By witchcraft to the marriage bed.

The rhetoric here comes straight out of the Malleus Maleficarum, *or
"*Hammer of the Witches,*" the treatise on the prosecution of witches
that Innocent allowed to be used, for a few years, as a basis for trials in
the secular courts of Europe. You could consider this a cautious, qualified
endorsement at one remove from the Inquisition (there may have been
some natural suspicion about its efficacy because two German clergymen,
Heinrich Kramer and Jacob Sprenger, claimed authorship and no clerics
north of the Po could be trusted). If the Pope's son wanted to use such a
treatise as a way to legitimize his own particular approach to his
campaigns, well ... what mattered were results.*

    *Reading this now, I realize I was probably too immersed in those
influences of Medici's private circle (such as Pico della Mirandola's
neo-Platonism). I had come to believe Medici's genius was in his veiled
counterplot to undermine the Papal authority by licensing the worst
kind of mob rule and forcing the Vatican's hand by how far it would
exercise its power in city states where its influence was waning.*

    I was reading far too much into how the Malleus *came into being. I
was presuming that the sophistication of conspiracies and counterplots
of that era was equal to my own. Perhaps I was sentimental about
history, but I attributed nobler intentions and fewer machinations in
the secular courts.*

Gethsemane, as soon as he
Had entered, had begun to think
Of how his influence might be
Of value, though she loathed to sink
So low to ask of any man
What she might need, and show her hand.
With such a dance of motives there
Were steps requiring grace; she cared
More than he'd know about her claim

To stubborn independence from
The sycophants whose power had come
And gone from Sforza's court, where fame
And favour soon enough revealed
The tarnished sheen, the dark fate sealed.

"I've come to you because I've reached
What seems to be a real impasse,
I know Andalus has beseeched
You for your knowledge in these last
Few weeks that we've been working long
Into the morning hours; what's wrong
With all we've tried, I had to ask
Myself. There is another task
At hand that's taken all the boy's
Attention presently, one I
Did not predict; he seemed too shy
For the attention he enjoys
From this young woman, come to sit
Each day; her portrait, bit by bit

"Has claimed his focus, she his heart
It seems, and she in turn looks quite
Content to play the lover's part
And lead him further on, despite
Her marriage to perhaps the worst
Of all the thugs the Pope has cursed
Us with, defenders of his throne
Who've left me, for a time, alone
Though both of us have seen enough
I think, to know the wind has changed
And in the silence now, a strange
Expectant feeling, that no puff
Of smoke above the Sistine will
Be glimpsed before some darkness still."

I was in Rome when Cardinal Pacelli was elected as Pope and took the name of Pius. I had gone down after dinner with my father to stand among the mob who filled St. Peter's Square. Everyone looked hungry, like they had come off a long train journey, though I could smell that talcum, the kind you only seem to get in Italy, on the women in their Sunday clothes.

I suppose we cheered as the white smoke appeared above the Sistine's chimney. There was so little to be hopeful about then, and from all we knew of Pacelli he seemed a clever old diplomat, someone who might even be able to keep the worst from happening. This was '39, the days when you could sense, from the martial rhythms of the songs on the wireless to the faces of the young men and women forced to march in uniform every saints' day parade, that the descent into the worst was inevitable.

From where I stood I could see the Cardinal Deacon emerge on the balcony of St. Peter's for the proclamation. He moved up to the microphone as if he was announcing a prizefight, so stout in his vestments, all he needed was a cigar stuffed in his cheek. It was the hint of menace in his gestures as he blessed the crowd and in the way he looked down at us all, with that flash of contempt, that gave me the feeling these men were no different than the sycophants of Il Duce who strutted around the Piazza Venezia.

"It's going to get very bad before it gets any better," Harry said, when we met later for a drink. He sipped his cognac and granted his flirtatious grin to the waiter at the St. Regis. Harry was, to my mind, the only man to be trusted in Rome. Trusted even by the waiters. Of course he was right. He was right about everything.

"I've seen this thug you speak of here
On more than one occasion and
He looks to be a man whose fear
Of women, long before he planned
To marry, marked him as the kind
Who, probably in youth resigned
Himself to play the hypocrite

And prayed, when he could stomach it,
For respite from his life at war
With all that he had to deny
As truly powerful, and why
If deemed madonna or a whore
He felt he could contain his rage
At life, and so play-act his age."

Precisely," Leonardo said,
"I fear his patience running out
And like his wife I've come to dread
His orders, all that they're about
And yet I'm weeks from any real
Completed work. What's worse I feel
I'm farther than I've ever been
From knowing what will yet be seen
From each projected stage along
This opus as this sacred stone
Transmutes apace, and I alone
It seems believe that we've gone wrong
With all the calculations we
Have made. We're not where we should be."

He fumbled in his satchel and
Produced the parchment pages they
Were working from, in his own hand
The progress he had scrawled each day
Where question marks like scattered hooks
(Enough to fill her stack of books)
Had turned each paragraph into
An inquiry to find the true
Alchemist's basis of belief,
As if no principle discussed
Had merited his sense of trust
And all the signs, however brief
Of progress hardly could provide

Assurances he'd now abide.

She studied these notes line by line,
Her fingers moving through the words,
For some misstep that she could find
Recorded, where the fault occurred,
Until, some pages in, she paused
And turned to him and said, "What caused
You to abandon what has long
Been deemed as praxis? This is wrong."
Her blackened finger stabbed a line,
She shook her head and huffed a sigh.
"These elements are male, so why
Would you believe they'd be combined?
Andalus surely didn't say
That I advised it works this way."

"He understood what were the rules,"
He blurted out. "I chose to cut
Through all this ritual that fools
The eager-to-be-faithful, shuts
The gullible into this state
Of piety, beyond debate
And deeper questioning of all
I understand that you would call
A sacred practice – I just can't
Take on such faith. Perhaps I'm now
Inured to that impulse to bow
Before some other cause that plants
Its foot upon the neck of truth;
Had too much of that in my youth."

"And yet you'll work without a twinge
Of guilt or second thought for those
Whose power and claim to riches hinge
Upon what every peasant knows

Can never justify its claim
To acting in the holy name
Of God," she said, then realized
She'd raised her voice, so exercised
She seemed the picture of a shrew.
She shook her head and tried to smile
And show that she could reconcile
And not reject outright each new
Approach – she hated how her age
Had made her prone to spite and rage.

"Apologies. Sometimes I fear
That I have taken on the worst
Pedantic attributes your peers
Who court great favour and have cursed
Us with this grim, benighted state
Of inquiry, and yes, debate,
Would happily maintain and claim
As necessary, in the name
Of some dark state of forced accord,
Transactional at best
And yet enduring to suggest
To those who'd raise both sail and sword
And launch attacks upon our shores.
This faith finds purpose in its wars.

"Enough on that though; what I want
To offer, if I may, is that
This practice isn't one to flaunt
Abstraction, despite all you've sat
And pondered on, I'm sure. It's based
On what can never be erased,
Employed to serve impure desires
Or seized and thrown into the fires
The agents of this Nero in
A papal crown believe will burn

With such unholy force to turn
Each childlike soul away from sin.
Each principle, set down, defined,
Is based on nature's grand design."

Her guest could only nod and smile
At this, content to have her think
That he had let his aims defile
Her faith, this well where virtue drinks,
Intoxicated like a youth
In love with how the force of truth
Can make a poet of a fool.
It would not be his role to school
Her on how many times he'd made
A mockery of doctrinaire
Inquiry and the learned air
Of those who so prosaic, staid,
Had placed such rules along his path,
And cursed this tiresome polymath.

"Allow me to say you're assured
You won't be forced to deal with those
Who'll take up arms in this absurd
Campaign it's futile to oppose.
I offer you my studio
To work, and share all that you know,
Put paid to this pretense the boy
Maintains while he's in my employ
That all that you've provided are
Some scraps of knowledge that fill in
The gaps that he could not begin
To comprehend in fact, so far
Is he from what his father claimed
To know that he cannot be blamed."

"You know that Sforza has his spies

– And no doubt Innocent as well –
Employed, with ever watchful eyes
Upon you. Soon enough they'll tell
Of this old crone, who every day
Comes to your studio, and they
Will find a way to figure out
Just what my visits are about
And this will draw attention to
A lot more than the work you're paid
To do, or how you have portrayed
Yourself. This won't be good for you.
I may be over-cautious, but
One trusts the feelings from the gut."

He nodded, gathered up his notes
And smiled as if with some relief.
His words of thanks, stuck in his throat,
He'd finally spoken. In so brief
A moment he had made contact
With someone more than just transact
Some quid pro quo arrangement where
Each party didn't really care
What kind of soul was glimpsed within
The light that flickered in these eyes.
"I'm looking forward to your wise
And learned counsel. We'll begin
Tomorrow, if you can …" He bowed
Then turned from her, unmoved and proud.

Citrinitas

PART III

*Maddalena informs Lorenzo she is carrying
Andalus's child. They speak of what she must do to maintain the
honour of the family name.*

The worst of all that now had come
To weigh on Maddalena's mind
Was how she felt so exiled from
Herself and those that she defined
As making up her private world,
Who, since she was a little girl
Had kept her safe from consequence.
"One who confesses and repents,"
Her mother told her long ago,
"Can say that they've removed each stain
Upon the soul and have maintained
A house in order and can show
Each well-lit room within her for
The world to see, with open door."

Yet what occurred within a small
Dark chamber pierced, a single ray
Of light, this state of grace. And all
Within no longer seemed the way

It was. The shadows now consumed
In darkness any hope these rooms
Would ever be the same. A door
Had closed upon the past. No more
Could she portray the ingenue
She'd been. All that remained of her
Was just a portrait that could blur
Her past into her present; few
Among those who defined her life
Could say they saw the child ... the wife ...

For now another woman seemed
To be revealed in gilded frame.
Her eyes had something of the gleam
That would betray her with the name
Of love, exposing her as one
Who'd broken every vow, undone
By a seduction based upon
The knowledge it could not go on
If she had any true belief
In who she once had been, the role
She played before this painter stole
The mask she fashioned, that no grief
Or private yearning could have marred –
That mask now looked like it was scarred.

She only had one place to go,
She knew, where she could bare her soul.
Her father, though enraged, would know
What she could keep in her control
And what she'd have to sacrifice
To fate, for more than just advice
He would be able to provide.
He knew the widening divide
Between her and Cybo appeared
Upon the very day they wed

And not unlike the marriage bed
He and her mother had for years
Abandoned, he could understand
How love could snap a wedding band.

She waited for the moment when,
While at the court of Sforza, she
Could take his hand while gentlemen
With brittle choreography
Approached their ladies for the dance
That closed the masque, therein the chance
To have him now perform as well
As father proud, so all could tell
With such theatrics, how he chose
This celebration, solely planned
To maintain the firm command
Of his empire. Here he supposed
She'd be content and dutiful,
A cipher of the beautiful.

But beauty had its own remit
To be considered, that he'd seemed
Reluctant to accept, admit
And factor in all that he schemed
Without as much as just a look
Her way while speaking, as he took
For granted her devotion to
A legacy she had to view
As their responsibility.
So much assumed; so much denied,
But worse, so much he never tried
To understand – "fragility"
Was what he deemed her tragic flaw –
A heart ruled by its broken laws.

If I was seeing anything on stage as I wrote these scenes, it was not some nod to the theatre of my sister's crowd. It was closer to opera (but, yes, one whose set was designed by Bacon). You will remember there is a ballroom scene in Eugene Onegin. *I had vivid memories of seeing it at Covent Garden with my mother and father as a child. To sit there in the dark and to see the tears streaming down my mother's face by the third act, I felt as if I could sense the depth of her terminal homesickness for the Russia she'd left behind – the Russia that no longer existed, of course. That is when I first fell in love with Tchaikovsky's music. I had the phonograph recordings in London that I would listen to as I plodded through these verses. If I have any regret about the few years I spent scribbling away, it is that I did not try to write a libretto while I still had some ambition. That would have actually given me some pleasure, I think.*

But far from broken and unbowed
Was her determined state of mind.
No treacly sentiments would cloud
Her judgment, her father now would find.
She took him by the hand and led
Him to a spot where what she said
In something like a whisper would
Not be revealed or understood
By anyone but him. The doors
That led out to a terrace she
Had in her sights and he could see
All those around them were ignored;
Such was her simmering urgency
To share her heart's delinquency.

He smiled and nodded for the crowd
Who streamed around them, too polite
To look surprised or say aloud
What they'd be wondering all night
About: what Florentine intrigue

Had put this innocent in league
With one less of a father than
This cool and calculating man
Whose family seemed but a piece
Of masquerade that he employed
To make it easier to avoid
The questions that would never cease:
Was every word and gesture just
For artifice? What could you trust?

"Apologies; I had to choose
This moment to draw you away,
I think I have no time to lose
For what I'm now compelled to say,
And every move I make beyond
That studio is watched; the bond
My husband and I have is such
That when I stray steps from his touch
So deeply does he feel a need
To know my every waking thought,
It seems, that even here I've brought
Despite myself, a "friend" who'll feed
Him with the nourishment he craves:
These notes on how his wife behaves."

She then produced, close to her heart
Within the folds of silk and lace
The proof of young Niccolo's art
Employed for means his sense of grace
Was wasted on, though with these words
He didn't seem, with what occurred,
To truly know how far things went –
Or maybe those were never sent.
The fact remained this role of "friend"
That he took on required the sense
To play both sides for her defense

(And his in turn, heaven forfend).
She was a pawn, where every square
Left on the board would lay her bare.

Lorenzo brusquely took each page
In hand and with a measure of
Disgust transforming into rage
Read every word as if his love
Had sent these to another man
And had revealed some secret plan
That would ensure the worst defeat
For the Medici realm, replete
With enemies he called allies,
So deeply did he feel this blow
From one to whom he'd deigned to show
Such generosity. The lies
This upstart must have told to claim
Such influence … never again …

"He writes to Innocent of what
He claims is a seduction you
Quite willingly, when doors are shut,
Seem to allow, sure you're not viewed
By anyone who could report
How far you'd gone, for love or sport
With this assistant – 'Andalus.'
Tell me this can't be serious."
At this, all she could do was smile
Considering the years she'd tried
To make him see what he denied
Or simply never reconciled:
Her claim to seriousness of mind
And purpose – if not yet defined.

"Unfortunately I don't know
Of anything more serious

Than this, that like an undertow
Possesses this mysterious
Unbridled force to cast one far
From shores familiar, with no star
To guide a soul the darkened sea
Claims for its own. Love's taken me
And drowned me with its warm embrace,
Will not allow me to return
To who I was, for I have learned
This heart that I thought so debased
In marriage and my role as wife,
Is capable of giving life."

I look at all the characters here in this text and despite myself, merely by the mechanics of this plot, this Maddalena is the only one who makes a sacrifice for something larger than her own interests. She is the only one capable of real love. Is that the closest thing to real heroism in all this? Probably.

Here my metaphor may be obvious and a touch trite but Olivia made the case for it to stay in the draft. "I believe these words are from her lips." When I made the point that these lines could read like a bad translation of an aria, she just laughed and told me that I seemed to think only good taste had to prevail in love. "If you only allowed yourself to believe that clichés might have some deeper truth, maybe you'd understand."

"A life that's born of your deceit,"
Lorenzo sneered, "that you'd be wise
To sacrifice before complete.
You'd best surrender to what lies
Ahead for you, and for the name
And legacy that all will blame
You for disgracing; that's the cost
Of this dalliance, so much lost,
Not just for you, when all is said,

But everything I've tried to build
For yes, your family, what I've willed
Into existence …. All that's dead
If you decide this life outweighs
This trust, deserving of its praise."

She'd never seen him so upset,
And as he spoke she couldn't hide
Her sad astonishment; he'd let
His tongue be ruled by fear and pride:
The fear of what he stood to lose
And pride of what his name refused
To entertain as something of
A right she had, to know of love
As it was written not in books
But in the body, like a spell
That laughed at sin, the fear of hell
That legislated with that look
That Dante spoke of, when he saw
His Beatrice – seduction's law.

It overruled all pieties
And nuptial contracts signed to set
A course that court society
In its denial would regret;
But these were thoughts that moved
Like shadows in a stream, not proved
Or justified from what she knew,
Just intimations felt as true
And real as what she felt now stirred
Within this vessel, made of glass
That held all she knew of her past.
The glass could shatter with a word
From him that cast her out, alone
To face a fate as cold as stone.

"So what do you believe that I
Should do to make this sacrifice?
There's no one here. I can't see why
A quick solution won't suffice
For what now causes me such pain,
Unless you'd rather speak, explain
To Sforza and his charming friends
Who'd make you think their life depends
On knowing – every moment – where
You are and what you think of all
They proudly set before you, call
So 'very Milanese.' I'd bare
My soul to Franceschetto long
Before I'd tell them what was wrong."

Lorenzo now retracted, smiled
For wasn't she, the way her eyes
Just flashed, in spirited denial
Of living for another's lies,
The very image of him when
He was the boy who would defend
The sanctity of "inner truth,"
An idealism that his youth
Allowed him 'til, as childish things
Had to be put away, he took
His place upon this stage, forsook
The knowledge only heartbreak brings
And learned his lines to play this prince
With honeyed words that would convince.

"I'll talk to Leonardo. There
Will no doubt be a way to get
This done. All right?" Then with an air
Of tenderness he deigned to let
Himself reveal, he took her hand
In his; he could not countermand

The bond unspoken that he felt
With her, the way her tears could melt
The iciest resolve within
Him, how with just his touch upon
Her cheek, a deep connection strong
Enough to heal this wound of sin
She seemed to be compelled to feel
He now had made more feigned than real.

And as they both then sensed all eyes
Upon them, quickly they began
To stroll as if for exercise
And to comport with the Milan
Not met in Sforza's court. They chose
To move among the crowd, and those
They smiled at, smiled in turn, and made
Her feel less on her own; she played
The doe-eyed ingénue so well,
With beaming father at her side.
Both now relieved she would confide
In him, he'd managed to dispel
The worst of all her fears. And she
In turn unlocked his empathy.

Now when I read this, I realize how a sense of surveillance is pervasive in the whole work. Real conversations occur in the moments when characters do not feel the threat of someone listening in, and of course all of it is written from the perspective of Niccolo, the spy and double agent.

Here I was, attempting a little escapism with this Renaissance plot, not realizing how much of my own state of mind was in every scene. That constant threat of surveillance marks it as a work so completely of that time now for me. Whether it was going to see how the paintings were coming along in Tomassoni's neighbourhood or simply having a drink with Farrell, I never lost that feeling that someone might be watching or listening nearby.

In the end I was probably not wrong. When Harry was finally picked up, Longhi said he had heard the Nazis had an extensive file on him. It was impossible to put a finger on just who were the informants in his midst, there were so many accounts of meetings, transactions. That a couple of amateurs like Farrell and me would have survived the war and managed what we did could almost make me believe in the grace of God.

Almost.

Citrinitas

PART IV

Leonardo speaks of how Andalus has betrayed him.
The master dismisses his apprentice.

Andalus found the note within
His quarters and hurried to
The private rooms where, if a djinn
Was ever conjured for these few
Impossibilities that spun
In Leonardo's thoughts, no one
Would ever know. He'd heard,
In jest, the servants, long inured
To Leonardo's temper, once
Inveigh amongst themselves at all
These rules in place, and he recalled
That word " djinn" used when, like a dunce
He willfully ignored the books
His father gamely undertook.

But that all seemed so long ago
And now he finally felt no need
To question what he didn't know
Or if by long hours, he'd succeed.
He watched how, stroke by stroke, his gift

Of image-making seemed to shift
His shape as much as he could say
The work transformed from day to day.
For all this talk of alchemy
Here was a transmutation that
Had just emerged, while there he sat,
His pride as bold as blasphemy,
A sculpted figure from the rock
Of careful brushwork, lover's talk.

And so it was a different man,
One who had shaken off the last
Parts of himself that seemed to stand
Between his future and his past,
An equal, he believed, compared
To he who'd mentored him and shared
With him the paintings very few
Had ever seen; now all he knew,
The very limits of his art
He'd summoned from reserves within
Him, liberated from his sins
Of soul's omission and his heart's
Retreat; out from this chrysalis
Emerged this bold new Andalus.

Perhaps he should have understood,
Expected Leonardo to
Be well aware, yet now he could
Not comprehend at first this new
Formality, the brittle tone
Of this hello, the way, like stone,
That Leonardo sat, and then
Rose up before he could extend
His hand to soften, with a touch
Upon his arm perhaps, the gruff
Recoil, the obvious rebuff,

For what he never thought had much
To do with what he had achieved –
Such rage about the misconceived.

But misconception, in this case
Could only mean one thing: the shroud.
He'd made sure that there was no trace
Of how, to impulse, he had bowed
With Maddalena in those hours
That she'd revealed more earthly powers
Than the seduction of the eye,
Though really, he could not see why
Such hidden pleasures would concern
His mentor; they had only made
The painting better; she portrayed
Upon the canvas what love earned
In wisdom, with a knowing smile,
An icon for the "sweet new style."

As the writing of Ocular *progressed, I had hoped to evoke something
of that "sweet new style", contrasting the machinations and the cold,
inductive process of creating an icon that served political ends with the
alchemical labours of Andalus, as he attempted to do justice to the beauty
of Maddalena. To posit that true, romantic attraction first hits you like
a dart when you see the object of your desire was my nod to Dante seeing
Beatrice for the first time on the Ponte Vecchio. "Less Machiavelli, more
of the Dante that wrote of Beatrice" was my implicit maxim. The "sweet
new style" was the only style that mattered.*

Still, all of that was lost upon
The one man who could recognize
When, with the force of summer's dawn
A talent blazed before his eyes.
What blinded Leonardo was
His vanity; he thought because

His influence just had to be
So great on Andalus, the free
And weightless state of mind that those
So prone to be seduced possessed
Would seem absurd to one obsessed
With art's perfection, and opposed
By temperament to artifice –
Essential for a lover's bliss.

But here, as if a drunken state
Had passed and sunk the spirit deep
In melancholy, such a freight
Of disillusionment; so, steeped
In jealousy he'd lost his strength.
He couldn't look for any length
Of time at him once he began
To speak; his gaze went to his hands
That trembled on his thighs as he
Attempted to explain the cost,
The confidence that had been lost
In him, how things could never be
The same with them, that much was clear,
As painful as it was to hear.

"If there was one true thing I've said
Since you have been here in Milan
With me, I told you when I led
You through my working plan
For this, her portrait ... maybe you
Can possibly recall? It's true,
Some weeks have passed, but I believe
It's fair to say much was achieved
Before what currently concerns
Me happened here, while I presumed
That you and she were in that room
As chaste as innocents – I've learned

Since then how foolish was my trust
In you, but be that as it must …"

"Of course I can recall, but first
If you'll permit me to inquire
Of you, because I fear the worst
From all these signs that there's a fire
Of rage that's coursing just below
The surface of your mood … I know
Lorenzo recently was here. Did he,
Upon a viewing, think that we
Have gone so perilously astray
With all the hours of work that we've
Put in, and all that's been achieved?
I wouldn't know of any way
We could have changed the process or,
With each new phase, done any more."

"Is that as clever as it gets
When you believe you will evade
My questioning? Please don't forget
That my name goes on what you made,
Just as it has to stand with those
Like our Lorenzo, who now knows
The worst of what occurred with her
And you. It seems you weren't deterred
By my express command to keep
Your distance from your subject while
Your brush was put to work. Her smile,
The look that hints at secrets deep
Within her heart, now seems a joke,
A mere nod to the trust you broke."

Andalus nodded, bowed his head
And realized that " misconceived" –
This choice of word – was what had led

Him far astray, for he believed
That ultimately nothing could
Go wrong with what he understood
To be the rite of lovers, safe
From prying eyes, the rules that chafe
Against the freedoms of the young.
To take this meagre portion of
What barely could amount to love
And now declare it worse than done –
A child to reckon with, no less –
Confirmed who's cursed, and who is blessed.

For even if he was the son
Of a Medici any court
Would cast him out, the guilty one
Who scoffed at marriage to consort
With, not just any noble's wife,
But one assured to take his life
Without a second thought.
The consequence that he forgot
To factor in this episode
Was how much more would be at stake
Than just a portrait and a fake.
If triggered, Cybo would explode
In rage; like cannon fire, the blast
Would flare and scorch the shade it cast.

And in that line of fire was more
Than Leonardo's studio:
Lorenzo looked as if he'd whored
His daughter out; he had to know
Of what went on, for once the spark
Between the two provoked remarks
And whisperings – "There was that note
She sent!" So bold, as if to gloat
About her many liberties,

An attitude so decadent
And Florentine, the evident
Result of such a life of ease
With no care for propriety
Or Milanese society.

"I think I understand you now,"
He said, "I see where all this leads,
If she's expecting; I'd ask how
A fallen woman like her pleads
For any kind of life again
In marriage, or how I explain
This all away and we go on
Exactly as we were. Upon
My life, I never meant for this
To reach the state it has. You're right
To feel betrayed; without a fight
I'll leave, and now you'll hardly miss
My contributions to the shroud …
I only wish I'd made you proud."

All I remember of reading Stendhal now is his definition of decadence: to act passionately about something for which you do not feel or believe in. In my career with Vidler's such an approach was essential; it was the transactional nature of the work. Yet I always told myself that my ideals remained secretly pristine; I believed I knew what was authentic art and what was fake.

Of course Tomassoni and all that happened to him — or should I say did not happen to him — as a painter complicated this. He had too much painterly skill to qualify as some naïf, yet he had no sophistication at all about what his contemporaries were thinking through with this primitive alchemy within the frame. He probably never painted the same again once he left Europe.

Though if he did manage something close to what he accomplished for this "Othello project," how I would have loved to see that work.

*It was the one question in my mind that almost provoked me to respond
to Michael Tomassoni's postcard.*

"Forget my pride. Care for your own."
As soon as Leonardo said
These words he knew they cut to bone.
Yet better to be ruled by head
Than heart, for wasn't that, at root
The thinking that had made it moot
To speak of other fatal flaws
He might pretend would seem the cause
Of how Andalus fell from grace
With him? Yet still there was what first
He wanted to remind him of: "The worst
Mistake you made was you erased
From memory the one dictate
Essential for a true portrait.

"I told you to remember that
Each stroke upon the canvas was
A choice. No god or muse who sat
Upon your shoulder changed the laws
Irrevocably cast within the work.
Well as in art, in life. The murk
Of motivation that compelled
You to believe it could be real –
This coupling you knew to conceal
Before you'd ever call it love –
Was like a draft begun without
A plan – that you believed, no doubt
You'd find the deeper meaning of
With time, unbound by consequence
And foolish faith in your pretence."

"But ultimately, I'm afraid
Pretense will fail the best of us.

Just as this shroud in time will fade,
She will forget you, Andalus."
"And so will you?" He fired back,
With only armour still intact,
The shattered parts of him now sealed
Off from the world, his pride the shield
He'd bear, just like an errant knight
From some romaunt his father told
Him as a boy to make him bold
Enough to stand, prepared to fight
For all that he deserved from life:
His art, a home, and yes, a wife.

Now all of that a distant dream
He'd only grasp again, years from
This time and place, where now it seemed
He never really should have come.
"Of course I will, and soon I'm sure,
Just as I know that you'll secure
Your own position at a court
In time. You won't have to resort
To what I do to compromise
Myself. You've got the painter's eye
While I'm just fool enough to try
What no one else will do. You're wise
To leave, in fact, before I fall
From favour – which destroys us all."

Those alchemical labours of Andalus were what I imagined a Tomassoni would experience as his own education of the heart. Yet even then I doubted I had it in me to write of the wooing of Maddalena with any passion or commitment. Granted that I wanted to make of Maddalena more the agent of this seduction with the writing of the note to Andalus and her forward attitude to him in the studio, but throughout Andalus seems passive rather than passionate. He lets things happen to him rather than making things happen. Such an approach renders him feckless in his final scene; he is dismissed, his career as a painter no doubt irrevocably diminished, if not destroyed, despite Leonardo's flip assurances. And he just seems to walk away, fighting for nothing.

The truth that revealed itself to me was that Tomassoni, despite his precocious talents of draughtsmanship and working with a palette, was a source of frustration. He rejected thinking about the frame, the larger context and circumstances that led him to be manipulated into this scheme of creating a series of forgeries. He was, like Andalus, ultimately a passive figure with the crucial decisions in his life.

In this I would tell Michael Tomassoni that his father was probably just a man of his time and place. He left school and his family at thirteen and moved to a Rome headed into war. Overwhelmed by a sense of some mysterious past and of the beauty of the paintings and sculptures he was seeing for the first time, he found his own way of making sense of this chaotic city through his obsessive sketching in notepads and on scraps of paper at his uncle's restaurant. It was a way to accommodate the contrasts that caught his eye: the gleaming black helmets of troops marching in the street and the raiments of the priest at Mass that seemed as old as the pages of a prayer book; ruins lit up by the air raid searchlights at night, with klaxons blaring, and the early mornings so still, with the streets empty but for the sound of the bakery man's bicycle tires on the stones, the jets of water splashing in the Trevi fountain (yes, these are my memories jotted down, but grant me a little license). I know that words on pages, signs and billboards meant little to him beyond the range of fonts and colours that whispered, ordered, yelled or screamed to him in a confusion of messages, but letters carved in stone looked as beautiful as the lines on an old woman's face. I am sure he could sense something noble and timeless, something rooted in truth in the way the marble fingers of this Moses in the Church of San Pietro in Vincoli seemed to move through the tresses of his beard when I took him to see it, and nothing seemed as black and full of sadness as the black of the cloak of El Greco's St. Dominic there in the Vatican, shimmering like spilled ink against a pewter sky.

He was a man who probably would have been happiest – and

perhaps his talent would have amounted to work of real artistic value – if he had returned to Gerace in Calabria and lived as his father and his grandfather did, with the same rhythms of rising early, making the espresso on the stove, tending to his own garden and walking the perimeter of the old town after church as his wife sat and gossiped with her friends. That would have allowed him to let memory do its work on him over a couple of decades. All the discord, alien influences, and broken rhythms of living in the Rome of his youth could have filtered into his sensibility. As it is for everyone who bridles against being exiled for too long, had he returned to Gerace, he would have found himself resisting all he sentimentally longed for in his years away and he would have become something like the prickly, neurotic, failed cosmopolitan. He would have internalized his sense of exile; I know that has always provided some consolation for me.

I only spoke about all this once with Farrell. He brought up the subject of Tomassoni with me back in London, after Ranuccio had left Dublin, saying that "your man" was enraged by how this travesty of an exhibition of his work had turned out. Ranuccio was convinced that we betrayed him. He had depended on us to make of him the celebrated genius we told him he would become. But Farrell was unrepentant. "He only had himself to blame."

I disagreed. I thought he never would have left Italy or believed he could make a go of painting if we hadn't gotten his priest to convince him he should work with us.

"Ranuccio was a peasant and I won't sentimentalize him. He never questioned our authority in deciding his work was of value because he never bothered to reason for himself. I doubt the man had ever read a newspaper, never mind anything about painting. He was an incurious weekend painter who was cynical about everything but his own inflated opinion of himself."

"Did you never talk to the priest, Antony? Ranuccio couldn't read. You're right, much like the peasant I'm sure his father and his grandfather were, he just trusted in those he felt had authority over his life. He didn't have a chance. We owed him more."

Farrell blew out his cigarette smoke with a snort and shook his head.

He folded his hands in his lap, then tried to smile. A stain of fried egg on his trousers. Still the filthy Jesuit. "I don't believe in feelings of guilt. I had far too much of that as a boy in Ireland. There are acknowledged and unacknowledged errors of judgment. That is all. Ranuccio's case is neither one nor the other to me."

But favour seemed more than remote
To Andalus as he'd begun
To pack his things. The words he wrote
To Maddalena, all he'd done
To make her portrait something more
Than cold and quick commission for
His master's praise ... all that remained
Of his devotions now seemed stained
With failure. Best to walk away,
Resist this impulse to destroy
The remnants of what, as a boy,
Was all he could have hoped to say
Would one day constitute his claim
To having lived, ill-starred for fame.

Tomassoni's work did not go entirely unnoticed once it was exhibited in Dublin. There was one review in the Irish Independent, *but it was so terrible that I never mentioned it to him. Farrell told me the critic had spent a couple of years in Paris after the war, trying to be the next Jimmy Joyce and "had come back to Ireland with his tail between his legs," looking for any opportunity to decry the influences of decadent old Europe on the pure Irish sensibility. He called Tomassoni's work fascist kitsch.*

After the gallery show closed, Tomassoni collected the work that did not sell in the van of a friend he made working construction, Spanish Frank, "who takes nothing seriously and that's why I like him," he said. Spanish Frank was not just a sometime foreman on construction jobs. He had money in real estate around Sandycove, gambling friends who were lawyers, politicians, actors, and producers in the Dublin theatre world. Tomassoni told me he wanted to burn all of his paintings on a stretch of beach at Bull Island, a spot where he would often end up in the first months of his exile, drunk and homesick, but Spanish Frank managed to argue for three based on biblical scenes. He said he could sell them to his friends and split the money fifty-fifty. It was never clear whether he succeeded or how much Spanish Frank might have made, and he could have only been joking when he said that one of them ended up as part of a stage set for a play at the Abbey Theatre, but neither Tomassoni nor I nor Farrell felt the need to pursue the matter. Aside from the work that ended up in that shed in County Wicklow, Tomassoni made a little bonfire of what remained out there on that barren stretch of beach where he could pick out the stars in the sky.

He said he had realized he was a painter "not right for his times". It was only a couple of months later that he was on a boat headed for Pier 21 in Halifax, Nova Scotia, with one suitcase and forty-eight Irish pounds in his wallet. That was the last I heard of him.

Until now, of course.

Rubedo

PART I

Niccolo presents the shroud – the ocular proof – to Innocent.

Niccolo waited, poised, in Rome
For word of last rites given there
Within the darkened Papal home:
Two humble rooms, where doctors cared
And monitored him by the hour,
Aware that with his dwindling powers
Of consciousness each day could be
His last. They kept the time that he
Received such visitors – despite
The seal of the Medici on
The letter this one brought along
With a mysterious gift, held tight
Within his lap – to hardly more
Than minutes past the final door.

Once told how little time he'd get
Niccolo felt relieved; the less
He could explain, the more he'd let
The image he beheld impress
This man, who, even in this last
Enfeebled state still seemed to cast
A pall of menace over each

Encounter or impromptu speech
He gave on the occasions when
He looked around the table and
Intuited that his commands
Were merely flattered. Loyal men,
Were just another fiction on
The creaking stage he raged upon.

As if on cue Niccolo heard
An angry shout from past the door.
No doubt some trifling breach occurred
Of Innocent's routine, which more
Or less was what a child required
Until this wraith at last expired.
What looked to be a surgeon passed
With hurried steps and eyes downcast
While murmuring some medicine
He knew he'd have to find, and close
Behind a Cardinal in rose
And white now waved Niccolo in;
Unsmiling, silently he led
Him to the humble iron bed.

As he approached he tried to hide
How Innocent's condition made
Him blanch. This seemed a corpse denied
Its final rites, the fates forbade
His peace with God which, given all
That Innocent had done, his fall
From any kind of grace assured
So many sins ago, this pure
Resistance to the final breath
Of any recantation of
His trust in power – less in love –
It seemed would damn him to a death
More fitting for the destitute,
No blessings left to scoff, refute.

Reading these lines once again, I think of my father's death.

It was '66, just after Passover – which he observed; in the last three years of his life he went back to faith in his own quiet way. After my mother died and he had retired from Vidler's at last, he gave the house to Olivia and moved into a small flat nearby. It was there, on a small iron bed, that he lay in his final hours.

It was not a Cardinal, but a banker named Ray Danziger, just as regal in his pinstripes and polished brogues, but with hard little grey eyes like a gangster's, who waved me in to my father's bedside. Ray was my father's closest friend in his final years. They had met at the Westminster synagogue and got on, it seems, with that curious, sudden camaraderie that can develop between those who have lived such different lives and yet have come to the same place, with all the vanities, prejudices, ambitions and illusions chiselled away.

Ray waved me over. Admittedly I did not expect my father to say anything profound to me in his final hours, but profundity can come at you at different angles, of course. It can be in the layers of meaning of something uttered with a far more banal intent.

"You pulled it all off, didn't you?" my father said, with that flinty smile I have probably inherited in these final years of my own. "I'm proud of you." I did not ask him what he meant, precisely, but I really didn't have to. It was enough for me to know he was proud of all my scrupulously executed deceptions.

But still there was that voice of his,
A whisper, hoarse and cracked, that gave
An eerie gravity to this,
The spiteful smile of the depraved.
"Come tell me of my dear old friend
Lorenzo, kind enough to send
This tribute that you hold, as if
Your life depended on this gift.
Who knows? Perhaps it does,
Despite how little at this stage
Of my departure will engage

These faculties, delight what was,
Suffused with such profanity,
A soul stripped of its vanity."

Niccolo wasn't sure if he
Should smile or nod with reverence
Respectful of this anomie
While bored with its irrelevance.
His intuition told him not
To do much more than what he thought
Would quietly astonish, nudge
The folds so all could see and judge,
Allow the image, with its power
To shock the jaded of the few
Among this old man's retinue
Still in this room, while by the hour
They felt they could anticipate
His passing – it was worth the wait.

I realize now that this process of completing Ocular *was more than simply a meditation on what was real and what was fake in the alchemical process of making art, and it was more than a speculation on the birth of a new sensibility with both the politics of love and the love of politics. It was, in the slow crafting of line after line, to tell a kind of secret history, a task arduous enough to strip me of any notions I had for a literary career.*

Over those months and years working away, I realized I had written to entertain and that was enough. I had so little that could divert me from thoughts on what the rest of my life would be like after this war. It had reduced most of what I once found beautiful and life-sustaining to smoking ruins; so I found, in those few hours of escape each day, a process that seemed honourable because it was stripped of a young man's vanity. I no longer needed to be recognized as any kind of artist; I was just making a kind of music out of my own hackneyed way with words. I had gotten myself out of the way with the story I managed to tell – and that was the end of it.

And yet, I suppose I did go on writing. True, it was a very different kind of writing I began to turn my mind to, hoping to find in art history and criticism some legitimacy and influence with Vidler and within the auction house, but it was also a wagered proposition for my ideal reader, one that stated that, with all her money and her aspirations of taste, if she was attempting to inhabit an ideal, I could give her at least a rudimentary understanding of what artists might be up to when they took on a work.

Yes, there was more than a little vanity involved in that decision, too.

And it was the work that came from those ambitions, I would like to tell my father now, that I never did manage to pull off, along with all the other deceptions. Too much of the truth was probably necessary in the making.

But first among them to respond
Was Innocent himself, who let
A snigger, sounding from beyond
His grave, escape before he set
His eyes upon the man in full.
It seemed this winding sheet was pulled
From off his bones moments before
The blood had dried. Who could ignore
The marks of wounds, that solemn look
Of suffering withstood? It all
Took on that aura one could call
The spirit of the real. No book
Or painting that Lorenzo could
Have offered would have been this good.

"I won't deny there's something here
That I did not expect to find;
But more than passing strange, so near
Is how a darkness has aligned,
As water seeks its level when it flows
Along a plane, the spirit knows,

And senses in a work like this
Its latitude, as if the kiss
Of death had lightly brushed its lips
Across the work, and captured, in
The image, somehow deep within
This tattered cloth, a soul's eclipse,
The aura of a final light
About to sputter into night."

Niccolo duly nodded, sensed
A judgment had been passed, and yet
Was unsure whether such defence
Was now expected. He would let
A silence of respect prevail;
He knew that he was bound to fail
If he were to attempt to say
Much more that would prolong his stay
Within this room beyond one thought:
"What would your holiness prefer
We do with it? I could assure
You it in faith you'd rather not
Allow it to be shown, returned,
Perhaps to simply have it burned?"

"That probably is too severe
A sentence for what was, at base
A gift unto the Church. I fear
That such a gesture would erase
The sketch of greater plans we've made
To link the gifts of wealth and trade,
Inimitably Florentine,
To all that's sacred and pristine
Within our realm, just as the bond
Of marriage, with my son and his
Enchanting daughter, in their bliss
Defines an empire far beyond

Our years, so let this tribute stand,
Archived, but in the safest hands."

He motioned with the slightest nod
To one of those attending by
His bed, who moved as if a rod
Went down his spine, his hands held high
To take from Niccolo the shroud,
Who gave it up, then curtly bowed
With one eye on the door, relieved
To know that he at least achieved
The minimum expected – word
The gift did not offend the taste
Of Innocent, work gone to waste,
But would in time, this much assured,
Find use within a church in need.
Where art had failed, faith would succeed.

For Leonardo, art would always fail. It was considered by most of his patrons a mere pleasure, and that was not enough for him. This was my contention, best expressed by that lingering sense I wanted to leave with the reader about him. If he really could have created photographic images beyond this shroud, aside from this experiment, he would have abandoned painting completely. He wanted reality. He didn't want personal expression and the alchemy of image-making with palette and brush stroke.

And that was a position I could never really understand. Why be an artist if all you want to do is be "true" to reality? Reality is just there to be transformed. There is nothing more authentic than one's choice of artifice.

Yes, I wonder what that something became for Ranuccio Tomassoni, but I assume it was nothing like what painting had meant to him in those years. How could it have been? For that brief period in his life, he was truly alive, creating work that would rival reality – and whatever the "truth" meant – for the rest of his life.

19

Rubedo

PART II

*Maddalena, with the aid of Gethsemane, carries out
what ensures there will be no stain on the Medici name. The return of
Jacopo Corvo marks an end to Niccolo's ambitions.*

When Maddalena finally woke,
At first she couldn't recollect
How she had got there, whom she spoke
To, or what at once she could expect
To see when she arose and saw
What was behind the door. To draw
The blind and look outside
The window marked a new divide
Between the half-lit safety of
The innocence she vainly fought
To keep and what her pride had brought
Upon her, so convinced that love
If true, would never cause her pain
Despite what sense of loss remained.

But now such loss was twice affirmed,
Her father deemed her portrait done
And everyone seemed unconcerned
About where Andalus had gone,

Including Leonardo, who,
If what he said was really true,
Knew nothing of his whereabouts,
"A restless soul, intense, devout,
His faith directed to his art,
I think he felt his time had come
To make his own way, painting from
His inspiration and his heart
What could I do but wish him well?
Where he would go, he couldn't tell."

If anyone had cause to doubt
These words aside from her, no one
Felt bold enough to speak without
The sense that no harm would be done,
Considering her husband's new
Campaign, his much feared retinue
Of mercenaries, hired swords,
The best a true faith could afford,
Who now had eyes and ears employed
Throughout the lands the Holy See
Considered Christian, if not free,
To make of freedoms once enjoyed
By all the privilege of select
Few souls who bought the Pope's respect.

Now that the deed was done, her thoughts
Inevitably dwelt upon
The life and love she could have fought
For, all so vivid with the dawn,
And freighted with an irony
So dark – she feared the simony
That others had committed she
Had too – but she had paid with three
Unfettered souls to win her place
Within the heart of Innocent,

Her own unholy trinity
Of father, son, virginity
(for though she gave Cybo consent,
She begged him to delay the real
Unfettered terms of such a deal.)

Yet all of these half-formed regrets
Were banished by a knock upon
The door. Gethsemane had let
Her sleep for hours, and now so long
Had passed, she worried for the state
She might be in, and what, if late
When she returned, would happen to
This girl, who knew to tell a true
Account of what she'd sacrificed
To anyone beyond the trust
Of this Lorenzo would, unjust
Though it may seem, more than suffice
To jeopardize both of their lives,
With whispered guilt a court contrives.

"I've come to rouse you from your sleep
Unfortunately, though I'm sure
You'd fare much better if I'd keep
You here for one more day, secure
In knowing your recovery
Was well in hand; discovery
Of any trace of frailty not
A possibility, we've got
To have you seem the living proof
That all the flush of beauty in
Your portrait's not that touch of sin
That haunts these ladies here, aloof
And by their art, less guilty than
Perhaps their patrons, to a man."

Real beauty, as Caravaggio taught me best of all, always required the
dirt under the fingernails, the flash of crooked teeth in one whose eyes
glittered and pulled you in. I pursued it in my fashion, but I remained
as discreet as Maddalena. Thank God all that's over.

As Maddalena rose, her smile,
More knowing than perhaps she'd hoped,
Said this ordeal would not defile
Her soul; in time she'd learn to cope
With how her life would be defined
In marriage. She would play the kind
And worldly doyenne of the court,
Secure that she could flirt, comport
Herself without the risk her heart
Would be on offer anymore,
As wise and hardened as the whores
That for her husband played their parts
So flawlessly, perhaps, who knows,
Within these rooms – doors safely closed.

Beyond the momentary peace
And safety of this humble room
Both knew there would be no surcease
Of greater fears, for now what loomed
Was what preoccupied Cybo
Apart from any public show
Of statesmanship left to perform
Here in Milan, a quiet storm
Of dark intent, a summoning
Of forces for this new campaign
That made Lorenzo's cold disdain
Irrelevant. The cozening
Directed by the Holy See
Assured the course, all states agreed.

For Niccolo, who'd just returned
From Rome, could sense the change in air
Despite the confidence he'd earned
From both his masters. How he'd fare
With any greater role now seemed
Dependent on this darker scheme
That gave Cybo complete control
Of every force within the whole
Of Innocent's embattled realm.
He knew it best to wait, report
To Franceschetto, holding court,
Explaining once he seized the helm
Of Papal force there was a plan
Led by a certain, chosen man.

"I'm sure you're all aware of what
The *Hammer of the Witches* states;
With Papal Bull, the word, as cut
In stone has set the task, dictates
The terms of my campaign, but such
A mission, with its trials, is much
More than a gentleman well bred
Can carry out. This will be led
By one whom you could say has learned
The skills of the inquisitor
As more than just a visitor.
Deep in the underworld, he's earned
His honours and his accolades,
A piercing light among the shades."

Those present, which included both
Medici and his host now looked
Embarrassed to be there, but loath
To leave. It seemed they'd brook
Such pagan rites within their states;
They knew there would be no debate

About the methods of this feared
Inquisitor set to appear
With Cybo's nod, a little touch
Of the dramatic, as a door
Now slowly opened: there before
Niccolo's eyes was Corvo, much
As he remembered, with that grin
Of one well-paid for all his sins.

If he had changed at all, it seemed
A life of favour with the few
Who gave him all he could have dreamed
Of profitable work, eschewed
By those who feared the Church's wrath
Had set him on his current path,
Made him a wealthy, well-fed man,
A kind of artist, one who ran
A different school to cultivate
The talents of ambitious whelps
Who knew the Lord loves those who help
The powerful. His graduates
No doubt had learned his methods well,
To send the innocent to hell.

During the course of my writing Ocular, I was becoming fascinated by all
that Farrell was telling me about these roving, assassin-like characters in
Rome, many of them old soldiers who had returned from skirmishes in
the north or in the Holy Lands with one highly developed skill and no
other means of survival.

It was my contention that Jacopo Corvo was a kind of harbinger
for the age that was to follow the specific historical moment of Ocular
(c.1491.) His ascent through the strata of society, from the beginnings
of the work where he is a marginal character – a street criminal with a
talent for murder – to his status as a highly prized enforcer and inquisitor
among Cybo's men, reflected the darker reality of Medici's world.

I'm sure, in conversation, I would have rambled on pretentiously and suggested that it was the Corvos of my own time that would define the age after the war. The ruthless survivors, the "killers with secrets", as Farrell called them. They would be the new men of power once the war was finally over.

I prefer to believe he and I got that mostly wrong.

"I'm honoured to be here among
You all," he said and humbly bowed.
"For many years I've served and clung
To my belief that he who's proud
In his convictions, unafraid
To face the many who've betrayed
The Church and set him to the test
That proves his true beliefs the best,
Has written for himself a role
That will require great discipline
And fully sanctioned power within
Such rooms as these, where our shared goal
Of government in true accord
Serves best the church and Him, our Lord."

He crossed himself as if he held
A blade within his hand to seal
His faith in blood, or pen and spelled
His signature to sign a deal.
With both these gestures it was clear
That all that changed over the years
Since Niccolo had known him for
How he had evened up the score
And damned Niccolo's father in
The eyes of those who held his fate
Within their hands, if now the slate
Was clear, atonement for his sins
Was all a piece. Upon this stage
He played a man made for this age.

Niccolo wasn't conscious of
The way his manner told the tale
Of how, from loyalty and love
He could not stray, and he would fail
In any role that would support
These men, if even to report
Their progress to the dying Pope.
There was no way that he could hope
To do his family proud – and so
Because this murderer's campaign
Was but the work of one who reigned
To solely benefit the crow
Who fed on carrion, despair,
He begged to take his leave and get some air.

And once outside he breathed a sigh
Of deep, disconsolate relief.
Perhaps at heart he yearned to cry
If he could summon true belief
But no illusion could compel
Him to return; the road to hell –
Whatever that might mean in truth –
Was better left untrod in youth.
He'd happily forfeit his place
Within these halls of power if
In time it meant he'd serve his gift
With greater honour, and the grace
Of one who proved his worth in deed,
The work that, in time, all would read.

*And so Niccolo walks away from his duties to the ailing Innocent and
the last days of his regime. This is the last touch to the framing story
("Machiavelli's missing years," I once called it, almost seriously). This
summer of Lorenzo's time in Milan, with the creation of the shroud and
the portrait, gave him all the insight he would need to write* The Prince

years later. It provided him with the sensibility to understand states-
manship and the true nature of art in the service of the powerful – and
of course, power in the service of art. In his education was a pilgrim
mirror image of my own.

If this was fiction, maybe he
Would now meet Maddalena on
Her way, returning quietly
To where she never could belong –
Two outcasts who had learned the cost
Of power, but who hadn't lost
Their hope a better age could yet
Be possible – and they'd forget
These bitter, broken final days
Of Innocent's embattled reign.
Perhaps they'd bond, and she would deign
To tell him all, and he, amazed
Would set it down in plodding verse,
His poem, for better or for worse.

Yet this is mostly factual
Unfortunately, so these two
Would never meet; no actual
Encounter could, in any true
Depiction of the worlds in which
They moved once be inferred. The rich
Were safely kept away from those
Who walked the streets. The closed
Door of the camera would be
Indeed the last room where this girl
Had felt the sense the larger world
Was where a love might finally
Be possible. Now that was gone.
Alone, both learned to carry on.

Rubedo

PART III

The portrait is revealed. The death of Gethsemane.

The time had come, with all agreed
To work to keep these city states
Aligned, and any further need
To trap what fortune would dictate
Within the lines of any pact
Now satisfied, for this brief act
In the Medici drama to
Conclude. Lorenzo's retinue
Were all instructed to prepare
For their return to court at home
And now, with shroud packed off to Rome,
All that remained that he could care
To celebrate or recognize
Was portrait posed: "a father's prize."

This was at least how he referred
To it when he began to write
His speech, where every well-placed word
Would have to risk the tired and trite.
In thanking Sforza for his grace
And hospitality, no trace
Of motive other than the pact

They'd formed would be declared; the tact
Lorenzo had a special gift
For would be summoned and his smile
Would smoothen out how, all the while
He had been in Milan. The rift
For years they barely could conceal
Was not, in truth, about to heal.

While he wrote on just hours before,
His daughter Maddalena tried
To dress herself and paced the floor
Reflecting upon on what she'd hide
Within her heart, the loss she felt
Despite how piously she knelt
At Mass now, with her husband by
Her side, where he could carefully eye
Her manner and the looks that came
Her way, at best assured no one
Would ever be for her that sun
And moon and stars again. The framed
And finely rendered version of
Her was the last trace of that love.

And while it was prepared to be
Presented, Corvo knew no time
Could possibly be better. He
Had gotten word of one whose crimes,
Reported by a prostitute,
If proven true would constitute
A case that best exemplified
The threat of witchcraft, justified
The very thrust of this campaign
(The prostitute knew Cybo well,
And knew whatever she could tell
Him would ensure that he'd refrain
From finding cause to cast his net
Beyond Gethsemane's regrets).

And so, well armed, as if for war
Corvo descended on the place
Where if a man desired a whore
He could presume there'd be no trace
Of something of his presence in
The rare event the carnal sin
Had been suspected by his wife.
Such sins paled when this woman's life
Lorenzo proferred was compared;
For in the end, he'd sanctioned this,
The worst of Cybo's ludicrous
Designs, as Innocent's proud heir
Of this corrupted, spent empire –
He'd set the terms and lit the fire.

Gethsemane was given word
Of Corvo's dark intent and yet
Whatever horror now occurred,
She was at peace, prepared to let
Them do their worst, accept her fate
As proof that the pontificate
Was justified in its pursuit
Of pagan ways, and if the brute
Force of a Corvo was required
To rid the states of such a scourge
Then so be it; what would be purged
In all these so called "cleansing fires"
Was something like a secret past
That trapped the light in darkened glass.

And in the image cast within
The phantom figures of an age,
Enshrouded in such acts of sin
That few would risk words on the page
To tell of what their work revealed,
Resolved to silence than to yield

To Innocent's benighted reign.
Whatever final cries of pain
Gethsemane imagined she
Could be reduced to in the end,
Would just empower her to defend
That shadow world, where those still free
From Corvo's grasp would carry on
Undaunted, unified and strong.

Such fears for Leonardo were
Enough to give him pause as he
Considered all that could occur
If in duress Gethsemane
Revealed how much she'd worked on these
Commissions, and how all that pleased
The Pope and his professed allies
Could never have been realized
Without the knowledge that she shared.
Perhaps this finally would cause
Him to perceive the papal laws
As not beneath what he should care
About, if he had hopes to thrive
Or simply, as things were, survive.

Farrell had this saying: "The only true history is a secret history." He was right. When I read Ocular *all these years later, I can still detect all the secrets I wanted to tell, all that I have attempted with these memoirs. I just do not want these secrets to remain undisclosed after I am gone. Too much to atone for, I suppose. I would go one further on Farrell and say that in all true histories there is a need for atonement.*

Good luck in finding it, though. The past is as silent as she pleases with me now, as silent as a painting.

But nothing now could be reversed,
He realized as he began
To make his way to where he first

Met Sforza. A much older man
He was, but more than simply by
The years that now had passed – his eye
Much like his heart it seemed, had turned
A little colder. He had yearned
For fame and glory through his art
When he was young, but painting now
Was like a charming trick, and how
He once believed he'd stand apart
From all of those who came before
Him now seemed vain and nothing more.

If he could just be left alone
To work on what could still inspire
Him … who eventually would own
The work he did and who desired
His presence, he could hardly care.
He walked these side streets, felt the stares
And wondered if he'd learned to love
As Andalus had spoken of
The way that Maddalena made
Him feel. Perhaps the bitter streak
That made him cold to those so weak
They didn't care how they were played
As pawns, that streak he could dispel;
Not time but rather art would tell.

"When I was a child, I spoke as a child … when I became a man I put
away childish things." The war gave me the dignity of actions that spoke
of convictions – not simply ideals untested by circumstance. It had freed
me from a young man's vanity. I could not have cared if Ocular *was*
lost to time forever, once I completed it. At least I had been involved in
an effort I considered noble.

Yes, the noble work of trading in art forgeries.

Yet here it was, this portrait placed
Upon a dais in silken shroud
And all it offered was the face
Of one beloved for a proud
Indulgent father who, like all
Who now proceeded down the hall
Into this room, could hardly sound
The depths of a desire unbound
Within the contours of a smile
Mysterious and sadly wise
Beyond this daughter's years. Her eyes
Betrayed those thoughts that kindled while
She sat so still for Andalus,
Resigned that they'd seem scandalous.

Now finally present to behold
This work, attired in what she wore
Each day, she found it hard to hold
Her courtly pose, act thankful for
This token of the new accord
Milan and Florence would record
As signaling the final stage
Before a kind of golden age
Among the Pope's allies would come
To pass – at least, so said the speech
That Sforza gave, as if to teach
His invitees, who looked as numb
As Maddalena felt, that here
Was proof that "art makes goodness clear."

Words deeply felt if not believed
By all these sycophants within
The room, who felt relieved
That any tiresome talk of sins
Of pride atoned for, either by
These Florentines or those allies

Of Sforza, wasn't once again
Brought up, like Innocent's refrain
From when he gave the Mass
Upon his recent visit, hailed
As he who would succeed, prevail,
Though looking like this was his last
Appearance, barely able to
Pretend the words he croaked were true.

Much better to perhaps rely
On seasoned actors when it seems
A repertoire's about to die
Despite the shrewdness of the schemes
Employed to liven up the scenes
Performed. Lorenzo, so serene
While Sforza rambled on, now took
His place on centre stage and looked
The model of a statesman blessed
With fortune, faith and family,
Proceeding to, so solemnly
Perform his lines that would, at best,
Command a measure of respect
For sentiments all would expect.

"I'd like to thank you all who've come
And joined us here today for such
A humbling gift, a vision from
The hands of one we miss so much
In Florence: Leonardo, who,
It must be said, I'm honoured to
Consider more than just a friend,
Despite that, much like you, I tend
To take for granted that his eye
And touch of genius, here displayed
By how my daughter is portrayed
Are such that, though the hacks might try

To replicate his every stroke
They chase a vision made of smoke.

"For here are unmistakably those gifts
Of subtlety and insight that
Remain elusive and that lift
Each painting far above the pat
Assumptions of the philistine
Who's yet to learn that the unseen
As much as what's revealed in line
And colour must, in truth, define
The drama and the mystery
That captivates, enchants, enthralls …
I'll treasure this work after all
My memories, like pagan histories
Of better ages, fade to dust,
For only art, in time, we trust."

And with those words his daughter knew
That standing there for all to see,
Nothing remained that she could do
When, more from stubborn memory
Than any words her father said
She felt what she had come to dread:
A solitary tear upon
Her cheek despite herself, how strong
She'd been to now, how well she'd played
Her role. But she would not allow
Such thoughts of then to affect her now;
She smiled and played up the charade
Of daughterly devotion, strong
And proud; here's where she belonged.

Yes, thoughts of now and then. In 1946, Willie Maugham had come out with a novel, Then and Now. *It was about Machiavelli. Even those who still like his work rarely speak of it. Not one of his best efforts.*

He was working for MI6 during the war and had come out, upon
an invitation of Harry's, to a rather famous Christmas party held at the
Vasi villa in Spoleto. He and Farrell knew each other well. Antony, who
had drunk too much, began to speak of this work in your hands, almost
as if it was his own. He had insisted Willie read it and that surely, once
he had, he would have to try to get it published. Willie just gave me this
lizard-like smile, so full of condescension and said, "Yes, you simply must
send it to me, Nicholas." I of course never did. That Then and Now *is*
almost forgotten gives me some consolation.

Attracted by the falling tear,
The way she held this tragic pose,
The so-called genius standing near
Her knew he'd witnessed one of those
Brief flashes of the greater depths
Of Maddalena's soul. She kept
Her eyes upon the work despite
The sense that she would now invite
This clinical invasiveness.
He'd call it an epiphany
Perhaps, his sense of destiny
About his future work with this
Infuriating art revealed:
A smile that speaks of what's concealed.

This was my last speculative flourish. Here is the suggestion that
Leonardo, without what Andalus achieved with his lover's gaze,
would have never come up with the revelation that was Mona Lisa's
smile. The painting of Maddalena was the first draft of that work, one
which the astute careerist was canny enough to steal from for the next
commissioned portrait he would do. I know. The proposition here about
Leonardo is not unlike the one put forth about Shakespeare, that the
real writer of those plays had to be Edward de Vere, the Earl of Oxford.
A commoner from Stratford could have never written such a body of
work that spoke of royal courts, of Italy and of histories so remote from

his humble experience. He would have lacked the imaginative powers, the more penetrating empathic gifts of an aristocrat who had access to humanity high and low.

I don't think at the time I realized the irony of such a line, given my own attempt to enter into the hearts of characters so remote from my own experience. I would have been so much more successful with this literary racket if I had just written what I knew, some veiled confession or memoir, and made something like a commercially viable virtue of my limitations. Consider these notes an effort along those lines.

And so, with all the speeches made,
Pronouncements on the virtue of
The gifts of art, the tributes paid,
She finally could see this love
Be shrouded, safe from prying eyes,
And take her leave, apologize
To husband, father and her hosts,
And slip out of this room, a ghost
To those who once made up her life.
She'd navigate the years ahead
With her communion with the dead.
She knew she really could be wife
To only one man, now long gone,
But life is short and art is long.

The work concludes with a stanza that puns on perfect vision, and with the simplest translation of the Latin "ars brevis, vita longa" in its original Greek, which inverts art and life.

I wanted to go back to the original Greek of this, the phrase that has run like a leitmotif through my life, because techne, or craft, is a term that strips away the connotations of art that is there in the Latin ars. In the spirit of demystification so central to my designs with Ocular, *I wanted to lay bare the workings, reveal the science behind the icono-graphic – both the portrait and the shroud. What a prosaic ambition.*

Life and art, art and life. In the end I don't suppose it is possible to get a 20/20 perspective on this work, nor of my ultimate motivations for it. As it is with all of us perhaps, it is only the fictions that can provide us with resolutions for the secret histories we reveal.

Does that sound something like a maxim, one that would provide that ridiculous term "closure" to all this? Well, if I could tell one thing to Michael Tomassoni, I would say don't trust it. Don't trust any final words from a pimp of art forgeries and a maker of fictions.

Thank you to
Fraser Sutherland and Bernadette Rule.